A Traveller in the Narrow

D.C. Priest

Copyright © D. C. Priest 2020
All rights reserved.
D. C. Priest asserts the moral right to be identified as the author of this work.

This novel is entirely a work of fiction.
The names, characters and incidents portrayed in it are the work of the author's imagination. Any resemblance to actual persons, living or dead, events or localities is entirely coincidental.

All rights reserved. No part of this publication may be reproduced, stored in a retrieval system, or transmitted, in any form or by any means, electronic, mechanical, photocopying, recording or otherwise, without the prior permission of the author.

ISBN: 9798677853401

For my friends and family who have always supported me and helped me make it this far.
And my friend William Butcher for the beautiful book cover he made for this story.

CONTENTS

Chapter One   Pg 1

Chapter Two   Pg 9

Chapter Three   Pg 18

Chapter Four   Pg 24

Chapter Five   Pg 34

Chapter Six   Pg 48

Chapter Seven   Pg 58

Chapter Eight   Pg 68

Chapter Nine   Pg 74

Chapter Ten   Pg 89

Chapter Eleven   Pg 107

Chapter Twelve   Pg 112

CHAPTER ONE

My year long trip in the Westerlands really hasn't gone as well as I hoped it would.

Though, I don't think anyone could've known that a fucking civil war would break out during my visit.

Since I've been here, I feel like the Gods have been playing with me, enjoying my suffering; or maybe my good luck has finally run out.

When I first arrived in the city of Gormus, all my belongings were searched upon arrival; then, the guards took half of the coin that I had on me as an *'entry fee'*.

I guess it's the price I get to pay for the *'privilege'* to visit the birthlands of Titus the Great.

What a fucking joke.

If Titus could see what his descendants have done to his empire, I'm sure he would rise up from the Depths with an army of monsters and burn Carlen to the ground.

Might make for a good tale if it happened.

I could tell it to the Nords in the North, or maybe the Eastern Folk, or whoever's lands it'd be cheapest to flee to.

So, why was my trip in the Westerlands so awful?

Well, I started my adventure this year in the northern territories, visiting abandoned castles, desolate caves and barely explored ancient ruins.

At least, that was the plan.

The haunted and empty castles of legend, like the Wailing Watch, were torn down, the desolate caves were filled with miners and the barely explored ruins were swarming with Imperial soldiers.

The soldiers tried to arrest me on sight, claiming that I was a rebel, even before the Star Rebellion broke out, but one of the captains saw that I was nothing of the sort and let me go.

So, that was a waste of a month.

A week after that, I was staying at an inn in near the Boundless Hills along the western coast and, I shit you not, the damn place was haunted by a Wight.

For the past six months.

Six whole months?!

I'm so glad the damn innkeeper told me about that after I paid for my room and meal.

I'm so happy that I got to find this out from the high pitched, chilling wailing and the visage of a corpse visiting me in my room that night.

Had I not been so curious about why the place was haunted, I'd have cut the innkeeper in half, I swear to the Gods I would've.

Though, in the end, I did kill him anyway.

The innkeeper had listened to my tales as we ate that night and then apologised to me profusely in the morning after I'd been haunted by the Wight, begging for my help in breaking the curse. He said that the Wight had been haunting him for months on end and without reason, saying that it began when his wife passed away.

He explained that they hadn't had much business at the inn in a long time and his wife had suggested turning to magic, using it to draw in travellers and Imperial patrols for many nights in a row. The innkeeper told me he was against it but his wife thought it was a good idea and tried a demonic ritual which ended up killing her.

Perhaps other adventurers would've been sympathetic to him upon hearing that, but I already knew the truth and that this man was lying to me.

Wights aren't Demons; Wights are spirits and it takes great lingering agony for them to manifest.

I feigned ignorance, pretended to feel sorry for him and agreed to help.

He thanked me and told me where he and his wife used to live, hoping I could find something there.

I said I'd leave immediately and fix the issue.

He turned to go back to work and I stabbed him in the spine.

Premature? Perhaps, but any adventurer worth a damn would've known the truth there and then and done the same.

Wights don't haunt people in general; typically, they haunt abandoned places or places where they died after their lingering regrets or pain caused them to be unable to pass on.

That causes them to manifest; there is never a Wight at a place without reason.

For a Wight to haunt a person, it must have meant it was them that had wronged them in life, so I could guess the Wight's identity already.

I cleaned my blade on his clothes, drank his finest vintage from his cellar, spilled the rest, and torched the building.

With that done, I went to where his hut was and found it long abandoned.

In the backyard, there was a shallow grave.

I didn't dig it up to confirm who it was.

Instead, I offered her my prayers, blessed the ground where she lay, and I hoped that would allow her to find peace.

So, not half a year in and I'd already killed someone.

Not the fastest I've had to kill people on my adventures, but still.

I needed a break after dealing with that, so I went to the nearby city of Calatorn and stayed there for two months, earning some money from telling my stories and doing the odd job and favour here and there.

After finally putting the ugly business with the inn behind me, I rode off in search of a new adventure and, instead, found myself surrounded by four bandits.

A good start to my renewed journey, eh?

I killed them all but my leg was badly cut, so I rested in a nearby village for a few weeks, wasting more of my days telling stories and struggling to walk down the street without a stick.

Once my wounds were healed, I gladly said goodbye to the village and rode on to find my next adventure…which I never found.

I was resting in a tavern one night by the roadside when I overheard people on the table next to me talking about the Emperor ordering attacks and executions on nobles that had Star-blood in their veins.

At first, I didn't know what they were on about until I remembered reading about the Children of the Stars, a small number of humans in the Westerlands who were supposedly descendants of the Gods, able to use powerful magic whilst using weapons and armour made from metal that had fallen from the Heavens, hence the name.

The Emperor had apparently been attacking a lot of them in the last fortnight and this had angered many of the other nobles and many more of the peasants.

I had hoped that these days would pass without further incident but, like I said, my good luck had fully run dry and rebellion eventually broke out, but not before I had failed to start several other adventures in the Westerlands.

I would go to a ruin only to find an Imperial battalion there, sometimes even what was left of one, no doubt killed by rebels or bandits, and I would quickly leave upon seeing either sight.

I would be taking a leisurely walk in the gorgeous woodlands of the southern provinces, only for it to suddenly rain heavily, sometimes turning into a storm, forcing me back to my inn.

A couple of times I would run into armed groups of nomads and peasants which, now that I think about it, were probably members of the Star Rebellion, even if it hadn't officially begun yet.

I always rode away from then when I could.

When it had been officially confirmed that the rebellion had begun, I immediately bought the fastest horse I could find and rode as hard as I could each day, praying to every single God of every single religion of every single race that I wouldn't run into Imperials or Rebels.

I didn't, thankfully, and I started to hope that my luck might have improved.

If only the Gods were that kind.

After riding from the western coast to the eastern coast to the city of Yarthan, I found that there were hundreds of refugees from the southern provinces crowding the streets. I found a good inn and paid a hefty price from a room, leaving my horse tied up in the stables, and then fought my way through to the docks.

I had hoped that once I got there, I'd discover that, while it could take a while, I'd be able to safely evacuate on a ship to the Green, perhaps to Nordstown or Driesport past the Cracked Shield Mountains.

Sadly, like I said, the Gods were toying with me.

"By order of his majesty, Emperor Illian the 2nd, and of his lordship Lord Carthagus, all ships have been denied entry and departure from the city of Yarthan until the unrest caused by the rebels is over!" A guard yelled to the crowd gathered at the docks. "Should anyone be caught trying to leave the city on a ship, they will be executed immediately!"

I couldn't believe the stupidity of what I had just heard.

Are you trying to get killed, my Lord, your Imperial Majesty?

Now, I understand barring ships from arriving into the city, as there could be mercenaries, spies, assassins or something even worse on them, disguised as merchants or travellers, so obviously you don't want them coming into the city.

But not letting people leave, even to go across the sea to the Crystal Coast and Nordstown is beyond stupid.

Keeping all these people here, clogging up your city, making them more sympathetic to the rebel cause and, arguably the biggest mistake, making the citizens pay for their extra time here out of their own pocket.

As it's his city, Lord Carthagus would have to pay out of his own coin purse for the guards to work overtime and keep the city orderly, and he'd have to find a way to feed the people or else they'd turn against him very quickly.

I had feared that something like this might have been the case, hence why I had gotten a room at an inn before heading down to the docks, so, at the very least, I'll have somewhere to rest my head until I can find a way out of the country.

Tonight, though, after a long hard ride and the crushing disappointment over not being able to leave the Westerlands on a ship, I decided to do the most sensible thing anyone can do whilst feeling upset.

Drink.

Drink until I can't feel the pain.

Drink so that, when I wake, I won't remember a damn thing from the night, or maybe even the entire day, before.

To alcohol! How I love thee!

I sat down on a table in the corner, gave my order to the barmaid and gave her a silver coin as a tip.

Even after drinking my fill, my troubles still plagued me, even as the ale warmed my belly and soothed my body.

With a heavy sigh, I let my head fall onto the table with a loud thud, a nasty scowl on my face.

I have to get out of the Westerlands, and soon, before a riot breaks out in Yarthan or before a rebel army attacks the city.

But how?

If the port here is closed, there's a good chance that the rest of the coastal cities in the Westerlands will have theirs closed as well, and there's no way I could swim the distance back to the Green.

And I don't have enough coin to keep a roof over my head until the war ends, nor a cave I know where I could stay in safely.

"You seem to be troubled, sir," someone said, sitting in the chair across from me. "What worries you on this fine evening?"

...Who the fuck are you?

I looked up from my cup and saw a man sat on my table with me, dressed in leather armour, a short sword by his waist, and an annoyingly cheerful smile on his face; sat right beside it was a long scar on his left cheek. He had short cut blonde hair and blue eyes that seemed to sparkle, even with everything that the country was going through.

Gods, I want to punch him in the jaw.

I wonder if I'd be able to do it and not get kicked out for starting a brawl.

I bet the innkeeper would understand.

Look at how miserable that old git is and how annoyingly happy this twat is; even the guards would be on my side if I did it.

...I'm so tempted to.

How can someone this happy, this friendly, possibly exist, especially when the Westerlands are in the midst of a civil war?

"Who in the Depths are you?" I demanded, glaring at the man.

"Wiatt; yourself, sir?" The man said.

"What's it to you?"

Wiatt was taken aback, but he smiled and said, "I imagine you're not here to enjoy yourself, are you?"

I snorted.

"Ya think?" I sat up and looked down at my drink. "Couldn't be happier that this fucking war started, the docks are closed, and now I'm probably going to end up dying in this accursed place. So, yeah, happy as can be,

Wiatt."

"Trying to escape the war?" Wiatt winced and took a sip of his beer.

"That, and tryin' to get home."

Wiatt raised an eyebrow. "Whereabouts you from?"

"Wheatcraft, little village a few miles out from Nordstown." I went to take another sip of my beer. "You?"

"Titus."

I almost choked on my drink after hearing that.

Why in the Depths was someone who lived in the damn capital so far south?

"The fuck you doing down this way?"

"Travelling. Well." He grunted. "Was. Now I'm scared to stay here much longer, you know?"

"Well, welcome to the party, friend!" I raised my drink and he raised his to clink against mine.

We both took a large swig from our drinks and then slammed the mugs onto the table.

Huh. Maybe this guy's actually pretty alright, or maybe I'm drunk enough to think he is.

"Well, unless you know another way out of this place, then you might want to head back to Titus," I said. "Least there you'd have a roof over your head."

"I can't," Wiatt said. "My Pa would have me thrown in the stocks if I did." Then, cheerfully, he said, "So, I'm planning on heading to the Green myself."

"How you going to do that?"

"Simple." He smiled, looked around the room, and then leant forward and whispered, "Through the Narrow."

At that, I paused.

The Narrow; a place I had longed to travel to before I lay in the dirt, but one I had not intended to go for a long time, for there was so much, and yet strangely little, I really knew about the place.

I'd heard plenty of stories about the Narrow, of course; everyone had, but never heard which were true and which were false.

My old man told me that the Narrow was filled with gigantic animals that were as intelligent as humans, and that obeyed the people of the Narrow the same way a dog would respond to a game's master.

A passing minstrel that had stayed in my home village for a few days had spoken to me of a city in which people need never eat nor drink, sustained only by the magic running through the stones of the streets.

A former friend of mine who was a merchant that had been through the Narrow before laughed when I asked what he saw, saying, "All of it's just a big lie. Just fairy tales to drag curious travellers into the city to take their gold for shoddy goods."

Needless to say, I wasn't his friend for much longer, especially not after he tried seducing my fiancé, the bastard! Rot in the Depths, cunt.

I had heard that most of the cities in the Narrow were housed in gigantic craters and caverns, buried deep into the Pale Mountains, but I didn't even know if that was true.

What secrets really lied in that thin stretch of land that connected the western part of Carlen to the east?

What bits of the stories that I had heard were true and which were false?

And, more importantly, what stories had I not heard about the Narrow?

My inner adventurer leapt at the opportunity to go and venture through it, but the ale in my belly and the pain in my heart told me that it wasn't a good idea.

Why, you ask?

Because the only way into the Narrow is by land, either from the Green or the Westerlands and, chances were, the Westerlands border would be closed.

"How you planning on getting through this stupid border lockdown?" I asked in a hushed voice.

If Wiatt had a way to sneak past the guards at the border and into the Narrow, then I didn't want any pesky eavesdroppers to report us to the city watch.

Wiatt smiled, looked over his shoulder, then leant forward and whispered, "They haven't sent enough men there to properly enforce the border. I know where they've left gaps and we can sneak past them, even on horseback we could, and head to the Green that way."

Normally, if someone came up to me and made such an audacious claim, I'd never believe them, but, for whatever reason, I believed Wiatt.

Maybe it was because of the alcohol, or maybe it was because I thought I'd figured him out based on what he was wearing, but I trusted what he said and I could imagine the Empire would be thinly stretched to cover all of the Westerlands.

Now that I think back on it, a lot of the Imperial Legions were scattered all over the west, at ruins, at towns and forts, and patrolling constantly, searching for rebels. Depths, I don't even know if there are enough soldiers in Yarthan to keep order here, let alone fend off a rebel army should they set their sights on here.

"Do you not believe me, sir?" Wiatt asked.

Shit, I'd gotten lost in my own thoughts.

I shook my head. "It's not that, more…wondering the what and why."

"The what and why?"

"Yeah. What's the plan and why invite me to tag along?"

Wiatt didn't even seem a little confused, nor concerned, about the questions that I had asked.

Most people would be distrustful and suspicious of anyone who randomly came up to them and began speaking to them, especially someone in a tavern or inn, so I had to wonder; why did he approach me with such a good offer?

"For the what," Wiatt began. "I intend for us to ride at first light from here to Yacatecuhtli; it's a city partially owned by the Empire and partially by the people of the Narrow. From there, we will depart as if we're heading to the southern coast when, in reality, we will ride south for a mile or two, then circle east and past the Spiked Gates.

"Once we hit the sea, all land from thereon out is part of the Narrow and the Empire has no power there. After that, it's a simple enough trip; just follow the Great Stone Road, staying at whichever cities will have us and we'll be in the Green within a month, I reckon.

"As for the why, good sir." Wiatt smiled and, as if it were the most natural thing in the world, just said, "Because you looked troubled."

…Wiatt, are you actually a really nice guy?

'cause, if you are, I'm so sorry for wanting to punch you in the face before.

Ah, the kindness and innocence of youth; may it never fade away.

I remember many years ago when I first started adventuring, I was quite like that.

I would offer my services and advice to anyone and everyone; if someone looked troubled, frustrated, upset or disheartened, I'd ask them what's wrong and lend them my ear and whatever else they required of me.

Now though, my older and more cynical self still doubted Wiatt, if only a little in comparison to when we first started speaking.

But still, I wanted to believe in him, and his words.

So, I grinned, held out my free hand and said, "Sounds like something good might have come out of this place in the end."

Wiatt smiled brightly back, grasped my hand firmly and we shook on it.

"I look forward to travelling with you, good sir…?"

"Athellio."

"A pleasure to meet you, sir. I'm Wiatt."

"Well, Wiatt." I stood up and finished my drink. "Let us get a good night's rest and make ready to head out come the dawn."

His smile grew and he nodded.

It seemed that while my adventures in the Westerlands had just ended, my next adventure that would take me through the Narrow was only just beginning.

CHAPTER TWO

The good news; I wasn't robbed in my sleep.
Or killed.
The bad news; my head hurts.
I didn't think I had that much to drink but, turns out, this city's ale is a lot stronger than what I've had elsewhere in the Westerlands. When I woke up, it felt like a dagger was pressed into my forehead and, worse, my throat was drier than a desert.
When I got dressed and went downstairs to get some food, I asked the barmaid about the drink and she said, "Our ale here, good sir, is our own home brew. Made with secret ingredients that only the innkeeper knows. Says it tastes great but hurts like a curse in the mornin'."
"And my dry throat?"
She smiled. "The innkeeper spent months perfectin' it so it'd make people thirstier so they'd drink more."
Yep.
Never, ever, *ever*, coming back here.
Not that I ever intended to.
Thank the Gods I was leaving with Wiatt today, or else I might find myself drinking something as awful and as foul sounding as that brew again.
Maybe the innkeeper was an alchemist, or maybe he was just a bored old sod with more time on his hands than he knew how to use it.
Still, after a few mugs of water and a full cooked breakfast, I felt rather refreshed and cheery, more so than I had in weeks.
And, as if on cue, I had to overhear something to ruin my day just soon after it had begun.
"I heard that a rebel army is heading towards the city. Heard they number twenty thousand at least."
"Apparently, the Legion has been diverted this way, but they might not

make it in time."

"When are they meant to get here?"

"Less than a week, I heard."

"Shit! I heard it was at least two."

"Maybe there are two armies coming for us."

"Do the rebels have that many men?"

That bit I wasn't worried about at all as that was obviously bollocks.

There was no way that the rebels had that big of an army, let alone two, or, if they did have twenty thousand men, it was probably their entire force and not a single army of a larger host.

So, that bit didn't ruin my day.

"...Lads, that's not the worst part..."

"What's the worst part?"

"I heard there's at least one Child of the Stars among them."

This one, fucking, sentence ruined my entire mood in an instant.

As if it wasn't God-damned bad enough that a rebel army, maybe two, were heading right for us, but one, or perhaps both, armies were being led by Children of the Stars.

...

Sorry Wiatt, but I'm getting the fuck outta here right now!

Sure, it would've been nice travelling with ya, but goodbye forever!

I quickly finished my food and drink, paid the innkeeper, wished him well, went to my room, packed what possessions and coins I had, casually and coolly walked out of the inn, and then ran to my horse in the stables.

I fumbled to store my belongings on my horse's packs and undo the rope lashing my steed to the fence when I heard a familiar voice call to me.

"Good morning, sir," Wiatt said. "Fine day today, isn't it?"

...Wiatt, I like you, but you really, really, *really*, have the worst sense of timing, don't you?

And fine?

Fine?!

"Morning," I said. "Wouldn't call this a fine day myself, Wiatt."

"Oh? What troubles you?"

I paused, turned to look at him, dumbfounded and sighed. "So, you didn't hear?"

"Hear what?"

"About the rebel armies getting closer to the city." I continued untying the rope and stroked my horse's mane. "Some people were saying we have less than a week before they get here."

"I heard."

I stopped, turned on my heel, stared at him in disbelief and frowned. "You did hear?"

"Yes, I did." He smiled at me. "What about it?"

"What do you mean what about it?"

He titled his head, clearly confused about what I was talking about...I think.

"If the rebels hit this city before we leave, we're dead," I said.

"Yes, but we were planning on leaving today anyway, weren't we?"

"...Well, yes, that's true but-"

"So even if the rebels get here within two weeks, a week, or even three days from now, we will be long gone by then. Even if Children of the Stars are with them, it isn't our concern, is it?"

I relaxed a little and lowered my head, mumbling in agreement.

He was right, I knew he was, and I felt like an idiot for panicking this much, and I clearly hadn't thought things through. Still, my heart hurt a little and not just because my pride had been wounded, but because I felt terrible for the people of this city.

So few of the people here had a hand in the schemes against the Children of the Stars and their allies, and yet many would suffer, and die, because of them...

A part of me wishes I could do something but, no matter how much I pray to the Gods and offer up my services, I am but just one man and one man cannot make a difference unless he has power.

I looked back up at Wiatt who, even now, was still smiling brightly, just like he had been yesterday, and I couldn't help but wonder if he truly didn't care, or if he was just better at hiding his feelings than me.

Maybe it's because he's still so young that he can act that way and hide his true feelings.

Once, I might've done the same, but I can't remember if I ever did. As far back as I can remember, I've worn my heart on my sleeve, both the good and bad...maybe Wiatt wasn't that sort of person though.

"Where's your horse?" I asked with a weary smile.

"He's right outside," Wiatt replied. "When you're ready, we'll head off."

"Right. Won't be a moment, so saddle up, lad."

Wiatt nodded and left me to finish preparing my horse for the long ride ahead.

I double checked everything, the saddle and sack quality, making sure that they weren't damaged, then the horse hooves, then my sword and dagger, and then my own boots. If they fell apart mid-journey, it'd be hard to make it home with bloody feet.

I mounted up and rode out of the stable and Wiatt and I plodded our way through the streets towards the southern gates.

As we rode, my eyes turned to the people and buildings around me, even though I knew that I shouldn't, and my expression once again darkened.

There were so many refugees that even the space under the houses in the slums had people sitting and sleeping in them. There were few guards on the streets and even fewer on patrol, the market was sealed, and, in the distance, I could see and hear a large crowd of angry people down by the docks.

I put the image out of my mind and turned back to riding out of the city.

Whatever happens next, I have no part in it.

When we reached the gate there were still more people coming into Yarthan, and only about half as many trying to leave.

We got to the gates, paid the guards the toll price and rode at a quicker pace away from the city.

Once we were a few hundred metres away from the city, Wiatt turned around and said, "I imagine a riot will break out in Yarthan within a day or two."

"Aye, I reckon so," I said. "With any luck, it'll succeed, and the people will fling open the gates for the rebels in surrender."

"I imagine they will, sir. I imagine they will."

We said nothing else and rode hard, following the road south-east to Yacatecuhtli.

The further we got from Yarthan the more I feared for our safety, understandably so.

If we ran into any Imperial patrols, chances are we'd be arrested, fined or killed, or all three.

If the rebels found us, they might think us spies or agents sent to recruit the people of the Narrow to the Empire's side.

Or maybe bandits would ambush us along the road, killing our horses, robbing us and leaving us to die.

Maybe we'd even get attacked by wolves, or a bear, or a monster.

However, despite what I had feared, the journey was largely uneventful.

No Imperials.

No rebels.

No bandits.

No random monster attacks.

No…nothing.

…My inner adventurer was somewhat disappointed about that.

The most *'eventful'* thing we saw on our journey to Yacatecuhtli was a vast army of Imperials marching near the coast north.

"They are definitely marching to Yarthan, right?" Wiatt asked, uncharacteristically nervously.

"…Yes. They're keeping as close to the coast as possible so that they can't be hit in their flank," I explained. "They'll probably keep up that pace for another two hours before making camp. Speaking of."

I looked to the sky and saw that the sun was beginning to lower above our heads.

"Know any villages or towns nearby?"

"There should be an inn a few miles from here," Wiatt said. "If we increase our speed, we should be there way before sunset."

"Then, let's hurry."

So, we did.

We rode in silence for the rest of the day and, just as Wiatt had said, we found an inn where we could stay.

Nice enough little place, quite cosy, and we were the only ones there, aside from the innkeeper and his family. They all worked and lived there and were more than happy to have people to serve.

We settled in, paid for our rooms, drinks and food for the evening and, as the night began to set in, everyone was sitting comfortably together across a few tables.

Honestly, I had hoped that this evening it would've just been me and Wiatt speaking alone at our own table in a crowded inn, so that we could get to know one another better because I still didn't know much about him despite having been riding on the road together now for the best part of a week.

The reason was simple; during the day, we were too busy watching out for trouble and during the night we were too busy staying hidden from any night attacks. If we took our minds off keeping ourselves alive for too long travelling through a country like this, we could end up dead.

I had feared that because our hosts were so eager to want to get to know us that I wouldn't get to know Wiatt any better; but, like our hosts, Wiatt was filled with questions for me. About my adventures, the places I'd visited, the things I'd seen, the people I'd met, the stories I knew, the whole lot.

And I was more than happy to oblige them.

"So, what's the furthest you've ever travelled, sir?" Wiatt asked first.

"Hmm, probably the Land of the Dying Sun," I said, rubbing my beard gently. "I think it took me about a month by boat to reach the continent and I stayed there for the best part of three years in the end."

"The Land of the Dying Sun?" The daughter asked who I guessed was quite young based on her looks.

"You might know it better, dear, as *'The Eastern Province'*."

"Thought it was always called that by the people there," the innkeeper said.

"Ah, that's a common misconception," Wiatt interjected. "The Eastern Province was the name given to it by Tyber the 3rd before his failed invasion of the continent. He had, quite arrogantly, named it as if it was his own territory before he had even conquered it." Wiatt chuckled and leant back in his chair. "What an arrogant bastard. Never even landed on the continent before his army was destroyed."

"Did he not?" The daughter asked.

"No, he didn't," I replied. "Didn't think people this far from the Easterly Greens would know that part of history."

For less than a second there, I thought I had seen Wiatt tense up, before he smiled at me and said, "My father served as a librarian to House Stowall where he spent much time reading and teaching me about such things."

"A learned man like yourself this far from a library must be rough, eh?" The innkeeper joked to which Wiatt laughed.

"A little, I suppose."

"Well, doubt you'll find anyone selling books in the Westerlands until this war's over."

"Indeed," Wiatt mumbled. Then, he said, slightly louder, "What about in the Green, sir? What great things have you seen there?"

I smiled. "Too many things to name in a single night."

"Truly?" The wife asked.

"Aye. The Green is filled with all sorts of beautiful and wonderful things, many of which I long to see again, even if it is just for a moment."

"Like what?"

"The Onyx Tower of the High Elves. It stands more than two hundred metres tall in the centre of the Golma, the great city of the Central Lands. According to some legends, the High Elves built the entire thing with magic, carving and laying every brick with precision using their spells."

Everyone seemed captivated by such an image and I, admittedly, was too the first time I'd heard it.

A structure like that of that size would take years, maybe decades, to ever finish, but, as the stories go, it took the High Elves less than a week. A High Elf scholar I once knew told me that it took less than a day.

The Empire might not have been built in a day, but that tower might well have been.

"Golma?" Wiatt repeated the name a few times to himself softly. Then, he said, "I've always wanted to know something, sir, if you wouldn't mind telling me."

"Ask away."

Wiatt swallowed hard and shook anxiously, like a child confessing their petty mischief to their parent.

"Does the Head of Golmertha truly exist?" He asked.

Ah, I got it now, why he was so nervous about asking me something like that.

Most people I'd run into in my travels that hadn't gone to Golma believed that the Head of Golmertha, the Great Stone Golem, never truly existed and it was just a fairy tale made up about a gigantic rock in the city's park to scare people into believing the Dread Dawn was real.

Even though the Dread Dawn was real and Golmertha had definitely existed.

In the oldest surviving legends and records we have of the Dread Dawn, Golmertha was a gigantic stone golem that stood taller than even the Onyx

Tower, whose footsteps shook the ground so much that people thought an earthquake was happening. While few remember how the Golem fell, the stories that I heard was that Golmertha died during the last day of the Dread Dawn, when the Demons were thrown out of our world and he lost his life protecting us mere mortals.

His head, more than twenty metres wide, still sits in the heart of Golma in tribute to him and his kin.

Even I didn't believe wholeheartedly he existed until I gazed upon his head myself.

"Yes, it exists," I said confidently with a smile, lightly patting his shoulder. "I have laid my own eyes upon it and it is a beautiful, if tragic, thing to behold."

"Gol-mer-tha?" The daughter asked.

"Ah, perhaps that's not a story well known to these parts either," I said.

"Should it be one we heard before?" The innkeeper asked.

"Almost everyone I told my tales to in the Green knew about his head, but perhaps it isn't that popular of a tale here in the Westerlands."

"So it would seem, sir," Wiatt said.

If that's so, then why do you know about it?

"Perhaps it isn't that popular because to see the head, you'd have to travel to Golma and that would be quite the expensive trip for anyone," Wiatt thought aloud.

"Aye, I'd agree with that," I said. "Then." I turned to our hosts and asked, "What sort of stories or adventures would you most like to hear about?"

"Do you know any fairy tales?" The daughter asked.

"Fairy tales?"

The innkeeper smiled and rubbed his daughter's head. "She's always loved them since she was little, and always asks the bards we get here about them. She never grew up from them."

"Dad!"

The man chuckled as his daughter's face turned red, a sight I couldn't help but smile at with envy.

One day, I hope.

One day.

Fairy tales, though?

I leant back in my chair and let out a low hum, closing my eyes as I did.

Truth be told, few people had ever asked me to tell them such stories, mainly because bards were usually the ones who recited such tales. Tales of great heroes and legendary beasts, of long forgotten wars and quests, of forsaken treasure and cutting morals.

Most people, even little kids, were entertained enough by stories of my adventures, so I had to think about it for a moment.

What did the bards back in my old village used to speak about?

The Dread Dawn, the Goblins, the Ruins of the Dragon Mausoleum, the old Nordic continent at the bottom of the ocean, the Sands and-

"Niefraditti," I whispered. I sat forward in my chair and all eyes turned to me. "It's not a fairy tale, but it's quite a beautiful one, one of a woman of eternity."

"The Dragon Priestess?" Wiatt asked; I nodded. "I don't think I've ever heard any stories about her."

"Nor have I," the innkeeper said.

"I haven't!" His girl cried loudly, earning a gently smack on the head from her mother.

How bizarre. People this side of the continent know of the Dragon Priestess but not Golmertha, though perhaps that's because her islands are closer to them than Golmertha's head is.

I smiled at them, cleared my throat and began to recite the poem that I had heard only a few times, desperately praying to the Gods that I got all the words right.

Far from our shores,
Across vast seas she adorns,
Niefraditti; eternity, alone on the shore
For she longed for life so little she roared
For she, poor she, was truly forsaken
Doomed to live alone in that haven.

On the Five she awaits all alone,
For she is the one trapped there by the sea.
A beauty like her left there, such a waste!
For she, never she lost her chaste.
For there, they swear, she lives all alone,
Where she dwells, few truly know.

There, in a temple, carved in the mountain side,
There, a great temple though ancient she resides.
In chambers of water and stone, she bathes
Patiently, waiting, a soul as gentle as the waves.
For there, only there, she can feel at peace
Whilst waiting for her all pain to cease.

Waiting, and waiting, for the one to set her free…
Whom, she wonders, who shall that be?

Once I had finished, I closed my eyes and smiled sadly.

I had always liked this tale and yet, every time I recited it, I would always feel sad afterwards.

"Wow," the daughter said with a happy smile. "Thank you, Mr Athellio!"

"You're very welcome, child."

She nodded and then yawned loudly, not bothering to cover her mouth as she did. Her parents smiled warmly at her and slowly stood up.

"It has gotten quite late, good sirs," the innkeeper said. "If it pleases you, would you please retire to your rooms and we'll lock up for the night?"

"Yes, we shall do just that," Wiatt replied, leaping off his chair. "Goodnight, good sir and madams."

"Aye, goodnight," I said, and our hosts answered in kind.

Once they had finished locking the front and back door, they proceeded into a room into the back where I imagine all their beds were. While I was happy that we had been in good company this evening, I was still somewhat bitter that I hadn't gotten to know my companion any better whilst he had just heard me almost brag about the great things I'd seen.

Wiatt, few things seem to upset you, so I hope that this isn't one of those things!

"Thank you for the wonderful tales tonight, sir," he said to me; I immediately relaxed and smiled. "Shall we depart after lunch tomorrow?"

"Aye, sounds good," I said.

We both walked upstairs to our own rooms, bid each other a goodnight, and I made sure to lock, and barricade, my door using the drawers they had in the room.

After my last few experiences with inns in this country, I didn't want to take any chances, not even when our hosts were this friendly, hence why I didn't drink any booze tonight.

Still, I must admit, as I gazed up at the darkness above me as I lay in bed, that I feel rather happy for once before I go to sleep, more so than I did knowing that Wiatt was willing to help take me home to the Green.

I smiled and closed my eyes, thinking of the last time I felt this happy and optimistic about my life; then, she appeared in my mind, right before my eyes with a beautiful, blissful smile that I haven't seen in many years.

CHAPTER THREE

As planned, Wiatt and I left the lovely inn and its owners after having a nice lunch that was far, far away from the crap I'd had in Yarthan. It was so good that I tipped them extra for it.

Wiatt did the same, though a part of me wondered if he did so because I had first, but he reassured me later that he wanted to do it.

With our horses in good health, our spirits high and our bellies full, we bade our hosts good fortune and departed onwards towards the border.

And, just as bizarrely as the days before, we didn't run into any trouble on the road.

Well, strictly speaking, that's not entirely true.

We saw a band of armed peasants with a few soldiers in armour among them, who we thought were rebels, and slipped around them before they noticed us; even if they did spot us, they couldn't give chase without horses.

Along the path we followed through a forest, we stumbled upon the sight of a destroyed caravan littered with carcasses. At first, we were anxious and approached it with caution, tying our horses to a tree ten metres away and slowly walking towards the scene with our swords drawn. But, when we got closer to the scene, we realised that the caravan still had all of its cargo in it.

Confused, we looked over the corpses and saw a number of armed guards, probably cheap mercenaries given their gear, and almost twice as many bandits, only two of which had any real armour on them.

"Rebels?" Wiatt asked, inspecting the corpses.

"Nah, these aren't rebels," I said, sheathing my blade. I bent down and put two of my fingers on a guard's neck, testing his temperature. He was ice cold. I stood up and said, "Well, they've been dead for at least seven hours, probably more given the smell. Based on what their weapons are, refugees I reckon."

"Are you sure, sir?"

"Look at the weapons they had, lad." I pointed to one of the axes next to a dead refugee. "That isn't a war axe; it's an axe meant for cutting lumber. That one over there. Probably an old sword or bought second hand from a shady merchant for a few coppers. That wouldn't even cut butter, let alone flesh."

"Though it would still bludgeon, wouldn't it?" Wiatt asked. "Still, to think they would be so desperate as to try their luck against a merchant caravan. Depths, sir, if both sides were struggling this bad to kill the other, why didn't either one run away?"

I grunted. "That just goes to show how desperate they all were." I flashed him a bitter smile. "Hey, give them some credit; they killed all the guards at least." Wiatt bitterly smiled back. "I'll see what's worth taking; you get the horses."

Sadly, aside from some money from the guards' pockets, there was nothing I could salvage that'd be useful to us.

Disgraceful to take from the dead?

Perhaps.

But it wasn't good to leave all this stuff here unattended so that it never gets any use; far better I say to use it rather than leave it to rot.

Still, Wiatt and I did offer them our prayers before we left.

If we had the time, I might've considered burying them in a grave together, but time was not on our side and the longer we spent here, the more likely it was that we'd get attacked by someone or something and meet the same fate as them.

Based on his expression, Wiatt was thinking the same thing as me.

We hoped back on our mounts and rode off down the road and quickly realised that we wouldn't be out of the forest before night fell; thus, we decided to search for a cave or someplace safe to sleep in for the night.

Thankfully, we found a large, empty cave that we could rest in and it was tall enough for us to bring our horses into. We gathered some firewood, ate a small, but filling, dinner and then rested.

Exhausted from our long journey, and struggle to find shelter, we didn't talk much again before we had to sleep. Wiatt volunteered to take the first watch and, despite the niggling fear in the back of my mind that he'd rob and/or kill me, he kept careful watch and then woke me when it was my turn.

I also might have checked my coin purse after he'd fallen asleep just in case Wiatt had taken something; after all, you never know.

The next day, we rode hard towards Yacatecuhtli and were about a mile from the city before we stopped dead in our tracks.

"This...doesn't bode well," I muttered.

"Indeed," Wiatt said.

Even though we were quite far from the city gates, we could tell from here that there was a massive crowd of a few thousand people gathered outside the city.

The city was closed, no doubt about it.

Well, shit.

In our original plan, Wiatt and I hadn't intended to stay long in the city to begin with and had only intended to spend, at most, half a day there, resupplying our food, water and herbal stores before moving on but, alas, it would seem we wouldn't get that chance to now.

And that wasn't the only bad bit of news.

"If the city's closed, then there's a good chance they'll have more patrols out in the immediate area to look out for rebels and people trying to sneak in," I said; I could see a group of cavalry off to one side of the crowd of refugees; no doubt there were more about looking for rebels and whatnot. "Wiatt, how close to the city was your road into the Narrow?"

He paused and began stroking his chin slowly. "It wasn't more than an hour or two from the city, if I read my father's old maps correctly."

Shit! There's no way that they wouldn't have patrols that far out from the city.

"Fear not, sir," Wiatt said, smiling at me. "I made sure to remember several other routes into the Narrow just in case something like this occurred."

"Truly?"

"Truly."

Wiatt, you beautiful bastard!

"Which would be the safest to take?" I asked.

"The longest, I'm afraid," Wiatt said.

"How much longer would it take us?"

"Maybe a day or two if we hurry."

"Then, let's take it," I said. "Don't want to run into any trouble now, do we?"

"No, sir, no we do not."

And so, with Wiatt taking the lead, we rode onwards.

Honestly, at this point, I was far too busy looking out for threats along our path that I barely paid attention to what kind of paths we took, or even what direction we went. I think we went back on ourselves a little bit, then swerved down a dirt path towards the southern coast, but then we turned again and followed a road along the cliffside maybe two miles from the coast towards the border.

That night, we had no choice but to camp out in the wild and it was safe to say that neither of us got a goodnight sleep. Even though we could hear everything for miles around, the ground was not soft to lay on and it made us incredibly tense and anxious to stay awake in such a place.

The reason was simple: we were camping out in an open field, with only our horses and swords, in a dark night with no moon, and whoever was on watch could hear everything that moved around us.

A faint breeze brushing against the grass.

The soft run of a rabbit as it scampered from its hunters.

The distant howl of a wolf.

A hoot of an owl.

Every single one of these soft sounds that night terrified me more than they ever had before.

This wasn't my first time camping out in the wild like this, but it was the first time I ever had to sleep in the open with two armies sweeping the countryside, looking for each other and their agents to kill. If they caught Wiatt and I, there was a good chance that both sides would kill us even though we hadn't done anything to warrant it.

We wouldn't be able to beat them in a fight and there was a very real chance we couldn't outrun them on our horses, so, understandably, I was more worried than normal when I heard noises in the night than normal.

Fuck, I'd slept in haunted ruins before and not been bothered.

It was the longest, and coldest, night I've ever had.

Even when I had been travelling alone all of these years, I'd never had a night like this before and I never wanted to have one like this again.

When the sun began to rise, I never felt so relaxed and calm before.

Well, strictly speaking, that wasn't entirely true.

When I was at home with my fiancé back in Wheatcraft, it was always so soothing and relaxing just to see her face when I woke from my sleep. She's always so cute in the morning when she wakes up, cuddling me tightly and wanting to stay with me for longer like that before we have to get up.

I love when she's busy at work as well, making her potions or herbal remedies; she's always so happy when she makes a new one and after she helps tend to the sick in the village. When we first met, she actually tended to a wound I'd sustained during my travels and I asked her to teach me how to make my own potions and remedies.

As she taught me, we got closer and, before I knew it, we were engaged and-

As I thought back to her, my dear Sarah, I felt something pull at my heart and my eyes turned towards the ground.

Even though we were on a journey home right now and I could see her again, a part of me had a dark thought and, in an instant, it threatened to consume me.

What if we don't make it back home?

What if I died a hundred miles from home and my body was left for the crows?

What if, even if I made it home, she wasn't happy to see me?

What if she had gotten tired of waiting for me?

What if she had moved on, thrown me to the wayside like I had to go adventuring and then married someone else from the village?

...Why am I so worried about these things this time?

I've never worried about these things before, even though any one of them could've happened a dozen times over by now.

So, why would I-?

"Good morning, sir," Wiatt said, stirring from his slumber with a yawn. He sat up, stretched his arms high above his head and smiled. "Shall we depart right away?"

"...Yes. Let's do so."

The rest of our journey to and crossing the border...I honestly don't remember it.

We rode and rode and rode, and my mind swelled and swelled with doubts and worries about our future.

Shit!

This isn't like me at all.

Then again, I've never had an adventure go so badly before in my life, not even the times in which I was badly wounded.

I pulled back my focus as best I could to our journey and, before I realised it, we were there; we were at the border.

How could I tell?

It was simple.

The stone the road was made of changed.

It went from being rough cut and covered in moss to almost symmetrical and smooth stones.

If I didn't know better, I might've assumed that the road was paved not even a year ago. However, that wasn't the case as Wiatt soon told me once he spotted what I was looking at.

"The Great Stone Road in the Narrow is carefully maintained by the cities," Wiatt explained. "As it is their main road that people and goods can effectively move along to get from the Westerlands to the Green, it has to be well maintained and protected. My father once read an old book from a scholar who once visited the Narrow many decades ago, saying that not even bandits dare attack the people repairing and patrolling the roads."

"Truly?"

"Truly, sir."

If that's true, dear Wiatt, I'll give you every coin I have.

"So, how do we cross the border?" I asked. "Toll? Papers? Bribe?"

"Ah, there's nothing like that where we are right now, sir," Wiatt replied.

"Really?"

"Really. Most travellers pay a toll at the city of Yacatecuhtli, but only the Empire actually forces people to pay it as a *'Generous donation in recognition of your enjoyable visit to the Westerlands'*, I believe they call it. Or something similar, at least."

I laughed heartily and smacked Wiatt hard on the back. "Good thing you led us away from that place then, or else I might've ended up cutting down the prick who tried to charge me money for that!"

Wiatt laughed with me as we rode off down the road, out of the Westerlands along the once bustling trade route and officially into the Narrow.

"Once we pass that tower there," Wiatt said, pointing to a long since abandoned watchtower. "We'll have passed through the Spiked Gates and will have officially left the Empire."

"Wiatt, my lad, I don't think I've heard better words since my fiancé agreed to marry me," I said.

Normally, I would imagine that this road would be quite busy with people going into and out of the Narrow, either to trade or to visit people or places, but, with Yacatecuhtli, the main gateway into the west from the Narrow closed, there were few along it other than us.

Whether or not this bodes well for us is something we would have to wait and see.

CHAPTER FOUR

My year long trip in the Westerlands really hasn't gone as well as I hoped it would.

After a day and a half on the road, spending the night camped out in an abandoned shack, we were finally within sight of the first city of the Narrow: Chicomecoatl.

Truthfully, I did not know that this city even existed as none of the bards nor fellow adventurers that I had ever run into had talked about it, so I was under the misconception of just how many cities there were in the Narrow.

I thought that there were six.

Xipe-Totec, the City of Warriors; Itztli, the City of Gods; Atlacoya, the Dry City; Xolotl, the Burnt City; Toci, the City of Healers; and Oxomo, the City of Star Gazers.

When I told Wiatt that, he smiled at me and said that I had only named half of the cities.

"If there's twice as many, how the fuck haven't I heard about them?" I asked him, quite frustrated at my own ignorance.

"Ah, don't worry about that, sir," Wiatt told me. "Most people don't know that there's that many cities because they don't have as good stories about them."

"Explain."

"Well, sir, Xipe-Totec is the home of the warriors who stood before Titus during his Conquest and their skill was said to have been unmatched, until Titus bested them that is. And Toci's healing waters are something truly from a fairy-tale, wouldn't you say?"

"…True."

"So, because some of the others don't have as good stories as the others, they're forgotten about by most bards and storytellers."

I can definitely see that happening.

Why? Because I've done it when I've told stories and so have plenty of others that I've met in my life.

I mean, when I think back to my travels in the Westerlands, there are places, moments and things that I've seen that stand out in my mind more than others. Depths, I don't even know the names of a third of the cities and villages that I've stayed at these last few months, mainly because I've tried my best to forget the terrible times I've had in the Westerlands.

Aye, I can definitely see people forgetting the less 'romantic' or 'exciting' cities in favour of the more interesting ones.

And, just as Wiatt had said, the city we were about to enter fit his description perfectly.

Chicomecoatl; the Prosperous City of Farmers.

Until the word farmers came out of Wiatt's mouth, I was quite excited to see what kind of city this place was.

I think I have a decent idea now about what it's like.

A little part of my excitement for travelling for the Narrow died with that F word.

Slowly, Wiatt and I descended on our mounts towards the city. It was located at the bottom of one of the cliffs by the sea, with more open grasslands than stone or wooden buildings. Even from here, I could see people working in the fields and tending to large herds of animals.

However, that wasn't what stood out to me the most.

No, the thing that caught my eye right away instead was even though Chicomecoatl was a city, there were no walls whatsoever.

Not even a small one around any of the animals.

At most, there were rivers that might have been too deep for the animals to swim through safely but, apart from that, not a single wall.

There was a small stone fortress near a bridge that lead into the city itself, but surely that wouldn't be enough to defend a city, would it?

I mean, thinking about it logically, they could be attacked from all, and I do mean all, sides.

At the coast, they were vulnerable. The only ships that I could see in their docks were fishing rafts and cargo ships. If a Nordic or Imperial raiding party came at them from the sea, they'd be crushed within an hour without proper naval defences.

From the main roads, a single fortress wouldn't keep the civilians safe. It'd keep whatever soldiers they have safe, sure, but it wouldn't protect more than five hundred people for a month, if that. There might be another one on the other side of the city that we couldn't see, perhaps, but even then, would that be enough to protect an entire city?

And, even from the cliffside, they were vulnerable. A volley of flaming arrows would reach almost everywhere in the city and set it ablaze within an hour.

"Wiatt, what do you know about Chicomecoatl?" I asked.

"Not much, to be honest, sir," he answered honestly. "The records that my father found were sketchy at best. The city is thought to date from before the Dread Dawn and that it has grown quite a lot over the last few hundred years due to its farmlands. From what my father taught me, Chicomecoatl's grasslands are able to be used for farms almost all year long, though no one is quite sure why."

"Truly?"

Wiatt nodded. "There was a book I found written by a High Elf scholar called Alfyr the Wise who spent more than two decades in the Narrow and he came up with several theories about-"

"Two decades?!"

Wiatt seemed a little startled by my yell and nodded. "Yes, sir. He spent at least two years in each city, trying to learn the secrets of them and came up several theories for each, but he never came up with something truly solid. The best theory he had about Chicomecoatl was that there was a deposit of magical ore beneath the grasslands that kept rejuvenating them even in the harshest of weather, but he could never prove this theory."

Even without Wiatt telling me, I could take a guess as to why.

There's no way that the people of the Narrow would allow an outsider to come into their land and start digging and, potentially, damage their farms in the process.

Still, would the magic ore really keep the crops and land fresh like that?

"Lad, you said that this place was the Prosperous City of Farmers, right?" I asked.

"That's right, sir," Wiatt said with a nod.

"So, what, the city's just a merchant city then or something?"

"Hmm, that's not quite right. I mean, you're not wrong, but you also aren't right either."

I think my confusion, and annoyance, was very evident on my face once he said that.

"My apologies, sir, that wasn't a good answer, was it?" Wiatt mused with a small laugh. "I meant to say that it is a merchant city in a sense, but no one really in the city would ever call themselves anything other than a farmer. According to Alfyr's writings, the city's name comes from the fact that every single person from Chicomecoatl is, in fact, a farmer and yet, despite not having a proper government within the city nor any soldiers of their own, they manage to endure and prosper in spite of all that is missing from a conventional city."

"You're lying to me, right?"

Wiatt smiled. "I'm not, sir. I swear to the Gods that I'm not."

"But, how can that be?" I exclaimed. "You can't have a city without soldiers or a government protecting it, so how the Depths haven't they been invaded or conquered yet?"

"Perhaps they have." Wiatt pointed at the fortress outside the city limits. "Perhaps that fortress isn't to protect, but to occupy instead?"

Then, out of nowhere, I heard someone laugh near us.

"I imagine it is strange to Green Walkers," an unfamiliar voice called to us.

We turned to our side and, standing up from his field, was a farmer with dark skin and brown eyes, sickle in his hand, and torn, dirty clothes, smiling at us. Immediately, despite the fact that he was speaking Carlian, I knew that he wasn't from either the Green nor the Westerlands originally.

While not everyone in the other areas of Carlen were white skinned folks, there were few dark-skinned people among the Green or Westerlands. In the Green, the eastern kingdom was made up of settlers originally from the Eastern Province and, in the Westerlands, there were people with brown or black skin colour from the Sands, but their skin was a different shade to this gentleman.

How strange; to find someone in the Narrow who speaks Carlian so clearly.

Perhaps he and his family moved from the Narrow into the Green and then came back, but that was unlikely.

Few ever left the Narrow once they started living there.

"Good day, good sir!" Wiatt called to the man.

"Hello, fine Walkers," the farmer called back. "What brings you to our fair city?"

"Travelling to the Green," I answered.

"Forgive me, but aren't there easier paths to the Green than this?"

"Aye, there were, until war broke out in the west; all ports have been shut tight."

"Ah, I am sorry to hear that," the man bowed slightly to us. "Forgive me for speaking as if I knew better."

"Easy, friend," Wiatt said with a smile. "We took no offense. If anything, it is nice to meet such friendly people at the city given everything that's happening in Carlen."

The man laughed and smiled brightly at us. "I am happy to hear that, good sirs. I couldn't help but overhear your conversation earlier about Chicomecoatl and thought I could be of some assistance to you."

"If you could, that would be most helpful."

"Indeed," I said. "This might be rude, but I've never heard of any natives from the Narrow speaking fluent Carlian in all my years on the road. Did you spend some time in the Green or Westerlands?"

"I did not," the man replied. "I was taught by a retired adventurer who settled into our city when I was a child; he taught me how to speak the Carlian tongue from the age of five."

"That's very impressive. Is that adventurer still with us?"

The man shook his head slowly. "He passed many years ago, I'm afraid."

"A pity. I would have loved to have spoken with him."

"I am sure he'd have loved to have spoken with you too, sir."

I smiled at the man and then, like the idiot that I was, I realised that I had forgotten to ask the gentleman something very basic.

"What is your name, my good man?" I asked.

How the Depths did I forget to ask him that before we just started speaking as if we knew the first thing about each other, aside from where we were from?

"It is Ikan," the gentleman said.

"Good to meet you," I said. "I'm Athellio, and this is Wiatt."

"A pleasure to meet you, Ikan," Wiatt said.

"So, Green Walkers, what do you wish to know about our city?" Ikan asked.

"Is it true that all of your people are farmers?"

"Yes, every single one of us is."

"Truly?" I asked.

"Truly."

…So, it is true then?

I know that Wiatt had told me as much, but it is one thing to hear it from something that was written in a book and it is entirely different to hear it direct from a local who lives in the city itself.

"How do you survive without any soldiers, or masons, or tanners, or governors, or without any of the things you'd normally find in a city?" I asked.

"We do have tanners, masons, merchants, innkeepers, craftsmen and more," Ikan said. "But those are jobs they do as well as farm. I am both a baker and a wheat farmer myself. As your friend said, it is true that we are all farmers here but we are not just farmers."

"Any soldiers or guards among you?"

"None at all."

Truthfully?

"Truthfully?" Wiatt questioned, as if he had read my mind. "What about when a drunken fight breaks out?"

"They don't, for that would go against the teachings of the Gods."

"What about thieves?"

Ikan's expression turned bitter. "A few try to steal and they lose their lives for it once caught. It scares most people from doing it for the next few years."

…What in the name of the Gods do they do to lawbreakers in this city?

"Then, who punishes thieves here if you have no guards or protectors to keep you safe?"

Ikan smiled and pointed to the fortress. "We do have protectors, but they aren't from our city."

"Where are they-?" I tried to ask.

"Beast Warriors from Xipe-Totec?" Wiatt asked, cutting me off.

Ikan and I were equally surprised by Wiatt just then.

Was it a good guess, or did he really known more than he was letting on? If he did, why wouldn't he share everything he knew with me?

"Indeed, they are," Ikan said. "Xipe-Totec sends us soldiers to patrol our borders, guard all of our cities in the Narrow and maintain our roads, especially the Great Stone Road. They patrol the city and fields, punish what few criminals we have, and hunt any dangerous beasts that threaten us, but that is all they do."

"So, they aren't occupying you then?"

"Not at all."

"Are they paid?" Wiatt asked.

"Only in food and drink," Ikan said.

"Not in gold?"

Ikan shook his head. "Xipe-Totec does not covert gold like most lands. They value strength more than anything. Those pelts and clothes that they are wearing." Ikan pointed at a group of five soldiers who were inspecting a part of the road. "Are from animals that they've personally killed. It is more than enough payment for them to fight and defeat the strong."

...They killed those animals themselves?

Two of them were wearing helmets made from bull skulls, one had a cheetah's skin for a cloak, and one had a black bear for a cape with a hood and a brown bear for the rest of his clothes.

If there's anything I need to remember after today it's this: do NOT upset any warriors from Xipe-Totec if you want to live.

"So, they only value strength?" Wiatt asked.

"Strength and wisdom, for it is not just brawn that allows them to defeat great beasts like those they wear," Ikan said. "Even those that wear goat skulls as helmets will most likely have come from wild or rabid beasts that would have proven dangerous to anyone else to put down safely. If you intend to stay in Xipe-Totec on your way to the Green, then perhaps you might see some upcoming Beast Warriors earn their pelts in the arena."

"Now that is something I would love to see!" I cried, a large smile on my face. "Ikan, my friend, I don't wish to keep you longer from your work longer than necessary, so I will just ask one final thing; where would we find an inn to stay for the night?"

"Within the market area by the ocean; all of our inns are there. As to which to stay in, I could not say for I've never spent the night there before myself, but the innkeepers there know how to speak a little Carlian."

"Thank you for your time, Ikan," Wiatt said, nodding his head to him. "Perhaps we will see you again."

"I would like that." He then bowed to us and said, "Good day to you,

Wiatt, Athellio."

"Good day, Ikan."

And with that, we rode on into the city itself.

Though, calling it a city feels strange to me, more so because of how it was laid out before me.

Nestled between the steep rock cliffs above and the coast, Chicomecoatl had one main river running through the city that forked off into a few smaller rivers, each of which had busy stone bridges over them. I could spot lots of farmland closer to the cliffs and almost all of the buildings, made from both smooth stone and wood, were located on two main land masses divided by the rivers near the coast.

We passed by the stone fortress we had seen on our approach and crossed one of the bridges into the city itself.

We slowly rode through the bustling streets of the city onwards past many houses and several small temples, each dedicated to the many Gods and Goddesses of the Narrow, though I knew none of their names. The people we passed on the street greeted and smiled at us, which we returned in kind, children excitedly ran up to us and spoke to us in the Narrow tongue.

I wish I could say something to them, rather than just smile politely at them.

Honestly, this surprised me.

If I was riding my horse through any city in the Green, I would get stink eye from most people, a look of disdain from others, and the very, very, *very*, occasional woman trying to *'woo'* me because, obviously, a guy with a horse must have a lot of money.

It was that logic which lead many morons to try and rob me.

Being greeted kindly by people and seeing how happy they were to see us was a nice change, to say the least.

After trotting comfortably for about ten minutes, we arrived at another stone bridge into the other side of the city and could see the market laid out before us.

It was gigantic, quite unexpectedly so for a city whose population was primarily made up of farmers, and there were many different types of traders as well.

There were: tanners, weavers, masons, alchemists, blacksmiths, wine merchants, artists, and even more craftsmen among them and I could tell even from my horse that they were of a high quality.

It wasn't the kind of cheap and batch made sort of crap you'd find travelling merchants in the Westerlands selling in order to make a quick gold piece here and there; these were created with passion.

It would seem that Ikan hadn't lied.

This really does make a nice change from the Westerlands.

As we were passing the various stalls, we passed by a wood carver's and, as if I had been drawn to it by fate itself, I saw a painted wooden carving that was truly beautiful, and truly upsetting.

It was a beautiful woman sat upon a chair with long brunette hair, small emerald fragments for eyes and dressed in a piece of native clothing from the narrow, a solemn expression on her face as she stared off to the side.

That might be someone else to them, a great leader or maybe even a Goddess, but, to me, that was my most precious person in the world.

…Sarah.

I wonder what she's doing right now?

Or where she is?

Is she busy tending to our small flower garden like she always does?

Maybe making some potions or tending to someone who's sick?

Maybe's she's out shopping for food?

Or maybe she's with someone-?

"Sir? Sir?"

I snapped out of my thoughts and realised that we had come to a stop; Wiatt's hand was on my shoulder and he had been shaking me gently.

Apparently, I had lost myself inside my own head just then, again.

I've been doing this too much as of late.

"Did something catch your eye, sir?" Wiatt asked.

I turned back to the carving and shook my head. "No."

We started moving again and then something caught my attention.

Well, specifically, an entire fucking stall covered in shiny jewellery caught my eye after the sun bounced off them and into my eyes.

I went to cover my eyes and cursed under my breath, bringing my horse to a stop to inspect the stand more closely.

Before me was an entire table filled with fine jewellery made of gold, silver and obsidian, each encrusted with fine and rare gems, like jade, rubies and sapphires.

"Buy?" The jeweller asked as best he could in Carlian.

The edges of my mouth crept into a small smile and I slid down off my horse, handing the reins to Wiatt and inspected the pieces more closely.

All of them really were beautiful and no doubt very expensive.

"I didn't take you as a man interested in fine jewels, sir," Wiatt confessed.

"I'm not," I said.

I reached down to the table and picked up an onyx ring with a polished jade stone on it.

And it was the perfect fit for her hand.

"How much?" I asked the man.

He held up five fingers and I pulled out five gold coins. He nodded eagerly and I passed him the coins.

Was it expensive?

Yes.

Yes, it really was.

And this is why I don't buy jewellery often.

But, when I saw this, I thought it'd be perfect for Sarah and, well, I wanted to bring her home something she'd actually like for once, not just more scars for her to see when we lay together in bed.

I thanked the man, attached the ring to the necklace I wore and took back my horse's reins from Wiatt.

He didn't say a word about my purchase.

He didn't even ask who it was for.

After that, we toured the rest of the market, tried out some cooked lamb legs with strange, burning spices on them that we saw, went fishing by the docks and then found an inn to stay that could keep our horses in stables for the night. Thankfully, the innkeeper and one of the waitresses spoke a little Carlian and we were both able to order dinner and drink for the night.

We took a table in one of the corners and tried to keep to ourselves so, at last, we could talk with one another more in private. Well, as private as one could be in a tavern.

And, just as Ikan had told us, no matter how rowdy or drunk the patrons became, not a single fight broke out.

There were times when it looked like one might start, especially when people started shouting at one another, though I don't know what in the Depths they were saying, but, whenever someone was about to snap, they stopped and stepped outside to calm themselves down.

"Surely this place is too good to be true," I whispered.

"What is, sir?" He asked back.

"This city. Surely something has to be wrong with it, right?"

Even with everything we'd seen today, my intuition as an adventurer refused to believe that there was nothing wrong or disorderly with Chicomecoatl.

Wiatt thought about it for a moment, shrugged, and then said, "Aren't you just overthinking things?"

"In my experience? No. Based on today's events? yes. Well, I'd like to think that at least."

Wiatt smiled. "Surely, sir, you aren't thinking that this is all just a false front that the city has set up for more than a thousand years to trick naïve travellers or adventurers, right?"

"Nothing that outrageous, ya git," I spat, before exhaling. "After the things I've been through the last few months, I've learnt that there's lots of bad, bad things waiting for people on the road."

"Well, that was in the Westerlands, the Land of Never-ending War, not here. Not the Narrow." Wiatt took a big sip of his drink and then slumped into his chair. "So, just enjoy it and this feeling whilst it lasts. I mean, come the dawn, we won't be here for long, will we?"

"Why won't we be?" I asked.

...It happened again.

For not even a fraction of a second, I saw Wiatt's entire body tense and he lost his smile.

It felt like the entire room had gone cold and everything around us went silent.

And, in the next second, he was just the same as always and his bright smile was back on his face.

"I thought that you wanted to get home to the Green as soon as possible, sir. Do you not?" Wiatt asked me.

"...I do, but..." I trailed off and stared into his eyes.

"Then, we should not waste a single moment, should we? After all, if we spend more than a day or two in each city, we'll run out of coin long before we reach the border."

Why, despite the sound logic of everything he was saying to me, why was it that I felt like there was something very, very wrong with what he was saying?

It made sense, of course it did; every single thing he said made sense, so why did I think it didn't?

...No, it's not that...

It's like my instincts are screaming at me, telling me that something is wrong, or that he's hiding something from me.

...Am I over thinking things again?

Am I just seeing things that aren't really there?

Or am I just misinterpreting what I'm seeing and hearing?

"Do you want to stay in Chicomecoatl another day or two, sir?" Wiatt asked me.

I shook my head. "Nah, we shouldn't do that. Don't want to run out of gold before we reach the border; they'll probably want a generous toll for entry. Still, I can't help but feel like we'd miss out on something if we went too fast."

"Well then, how about this, sir?" Wiatt asked. "Why don't we travel as quickly as we can along the roads and time it so that we arrive in each city before noon, find a nice place to eat for lunch, and then explore the city until we get exhausted?"

I grunted. "What about inns?"

"We'll find one, no doubt in my mind about that. So, what do you say?"

"...Sure." I smiled. "Sounds good."

That night, we drunk and spoke with the locals that spoke Carlian until we both began to feel the impact of the drinks and needed to retire to our rooms and, despite how tense I was earlier, I was able to sleep peacefully.

CHAPTER FIVE

Just as we had planned the night before, Wiatt and I left Chicomecoatl pretty much as soon as dawn broke. We bought some food from a local man who was just setting up his stall in the market, gave him our regards and began a much faster ride out of the city than we had getting to it..

In order to reach Xipe-Totec within the next few days, we had to ride faster, especially because, while we had restocked our food and water in the city, it wouldn't last forever, especially not the fruit we had. And we couldn't afford to spend too much in each of the cities, so preserving our supplies was essential.

And so, we rode onwards and had nothing interesting to talk about.

"Quite a cool sea breeze here, isn't there?"

"I wonder how tall those mountains are."

"It seems that the Great Stone Road really is maintained very well."

"It's quite warm today, isn't it?"

"The sea is very pretty."

Honestly, this journey was a lot less exciting than I had ever imagined it would be.

I mean, I was still quite in awe that a city like Chicomecoatl could even exist in our world, and it was a beautiful place, but the paths between the Narrow were barren, if pretty and, after seeing nothing but gorgeous scenery all day, we quickly grew bored of it.

Though, having such a sparkling ocean to our side to gaze upon as we rode was fantastic and very soothing. Much better than riding across dirt roads or empty plains like we had in the Westerlands.

Usually, this part of the sea would have a number of large cargo and patrol ships in it from both the Westerlands and the Green but, now, there were no ships in the waters.

Or so I thought.

As the sun reached its peak and turned to set, Wiatt, who had been absentmindedly staring out to the ocean, suddenly pulled on his reins and called his horse to stop.

"Sir," he said, pointing out across the sea. "Whose ships are those?"

I stopped beside him, looked across the sea and, in the distance, almost at the horizon, were a number of galleys sailing from the east to the west.

From here, I think I could see thirty or so ships and all of them seemed to be war galleys. There might've been a few cargo ships among them, but I couldn't spot them from here.

However, even from this distance, I could make out the flags that they were flying.

It was a silver helmet with a jagged red scar across the right eye on an icy blue background.

"Those are Nordic ships," I said.

"Nordic?!" Wiatt exclaimed. "Doesn't that mean that they're coming to raid somewhere?"

That's what most people would think when hearing about Nordic war galleys coming towards them and, to be fair to the lad, he wouldn't be wrong most of the time.

"Aye, they're Nordic ships, but not regular Nordic ships," I said. When Wiatt looked at me confused, I smiled. "They're from Nordstown."

"Nordstown?"

I nodded.

"How can you tell?"

"The flag. It's not of Nordic design."

"It isn't?"

"Of course it isn't. I thought you knew of Nordstown."

"I know of it, sir, but not much about it." Wiatt turned to me and smiled awkwardly. "I thought that it was just a town with only Nords." Wiatt lost his smile. "But, guessing by your face, that's not right, is it?"

I could barely stop myself from sighing in disappointment.

I'd like to think that he was joking, but I don't think he was.

How in the world do you know about all the cities of the Narrow and not know what Nordstown is?

You amaze me in so many ways, lad.

"I'm sorry if I've offended you, sir," Wiatt said.

"It's alright, lad," I replied. "Just assumed you knew more of the world than you did. Thought for sure Nordstown would be a well-known place in the Westerlands." I sighed and slumped my shoulders. "I guess it isn't as famous as I thought it was."

"I'm sorry, sir."

"Stop apologising, lad. I just thought you'd found out about it in one of your history books."

"I'm afraid that it was only mentioned in passing on occasion."

"How strange."

Well, I guess I shouldn't be too surprised.

If I had no knowledge of Titus, the damned capital of the Empire and I'd been all over the world, then it would make sense that Wiatt wouldn't know of Nordstown and its history.

I took a deep breath and then began my history of the Nordstown.

"Just moments before their homeland sank into the ocean, over three hundred thousand Nords were able to escape the island in a gigantic armada of more than three thousand ships and they sailed to the rest of the world. Originally, their intention was to come to the Green and seek asylum with the kingdoms there but, as they were crossing the Pale Ocean, the High Jarls began to disagree about the best course of action.

"One wanted to sail to the Dragon Isles, believing that they could take them as their own. Another wanted to continue with the original plan and find safety with the kingdoms of the Green; another wanted to invade and conquer the Green. And, finally, one wanted to find a new continent to settle on. They were unable to agree with one another and broke off into smaller fleets flying different colours.

"As a result of their actions, less than a hundred thousand Nords survived.

"The ones who attacked the Dragon Isles were all but annihilated by dragon fire; those who tried to invade the Green were broken and destroyed by an alliance of the kingdoms, and the group who wished to find a new continent to settle on managed to find one to the north of the Green, thus earning them their new name as the Nords of the North and keeping their people alive."

"So, what happened to the group who wanted to settl-?"

Just as quickly as Wiatt asked that question, he arrived at the answer.

He smiled, and said, "They found refuge in the Green and founded Nordstown, correct?"

"Essentially, yes," I said. "They arrive on the western coast of the Green, beseeched the King of the West to give them land and, after swearing an unbreakable oath to him, they were allowed to settle and found their own town."

"But it's a city, right? So why call it Nordstown?"

"When the Nords first arrived and started building their new home, the king decreed that they could only have a town to house their twenty thousand people. At the time, no one in the Green believed that the town would thrive and survive, thinking that only Nords would ever live in the city and, eventually, they'd die out if left on their own, so they jokingly named it Nordstown.

"Not a hundred years later, the town had expanded and grown to the point that sixty thousand people started living there and it became recognised as a city, if not in name but in title."

"So, why not just rename it to '*Nordscity*' then or something else once it began to thrive?" Wiatt asked.

"Because, lad, the Nords are stubborn bastards," I told him. "They named it Nordstown and they refuse to rename it. After all, the name has a lot of meaning for them, so they took quite a liking to it. That flag they're flying." I pointed back to the boats. "Was designed by the King of the West personally to represent the struggles the Nords had crossing the ocean and, to forever show their loyalty to the Kings of the West, they're not allowed to change it."

"Wow, I never knew that, sir," Wiatt confessed, completely stunned by what I had told him. "I feel most idiotic for just thinking it was called that because only Nords lived there."

"Eh, don't worry about it, lad. At one point, that would've been true. Though." I glared at the ships. "Why are they sailing to the Westerlands?"

"Maybe to conduct a raid while the Empire is weak?"

I shook my head. "Can't be. They aren't allowed to mobilize without the explicit permission of the King of the West, so that would mean…"

"They're openly joining the rebellion?"

That was a dangerous and ballsy move.

After Titus conquered all of Carlen, the Kings and Queen of the Green all signed a pact with him, naming him Emperor and their rightful ruler, and to forever serve him and his descendants. In exchange, they were given protection by the Empire and were allowed to keep their titles and original lands.

Meaning that, if the King of the West was openly declaring his support for the Children of the Stars, then he was essentially in open rebellion against the Empire.

"How bold of 'im," I mumbled.

If the Kingdom of the West was in open rebellion, then that meant that Sarah, everyone in Wheatcraft and in Nordstown could be in danger.

I had to keep that thought in the back of my mind.

I loved Sarah with all my heart but, if I started going down this path, it'd be all I could think of and that could get Wiatt and I killed.

I couldn't think of things like that.

Not right now.

We continued riding in almost complete silence for the rest of the day after that and we camped out in a small cave that we found for the night. We tended to the horses, ate and drank what we needed to and didn't dare overindulge ourselves in anything more than necessary.

Come the dawn two days later, we ate breakfast and rode much faster along the road to ensure that we reached Xipe-Totec before noon and, as a result, it wasn't much longer until we were in sight of the gates.

When I say gates, I do mean *gates*.

Xipe-Totec was built in a valley surrounded by mountains on all sides and, according to Wiatt, these gates were the only known route into and out of the city.

They were made of limestone and had immaculate, highly detailed and extremely beautiful carvings on them, with every part painted carefully and with great skill. There were lots of greens, reds and golds, and the carvings appeared to depict great warriors and monsters, but I couldn't tell who they were meant to be.

Another thing I couldn't figure out was how in the Depths do they even manage to close those heavy gates?

The gates to the city were wide open and there was a line of thirty Beast Warriors there, armed with weapons that I knew of, but had only seen a few times in my life: Macuahuitl.

A Macuahuitl is a wooden club with obsidian blades running along either side of it. It is a powerful, and very scary, looking weapon. They were also carrying with them a wooden shield decorated with feathers and animal bones, and no two warriors at the gates were dressed the same.

Even though we'd run into few people along the road, there were still plenty of people entering and leaving the city, each being carefully examined by the guards.

"Wow," Wiatt said, gazing up and down the mighty gates before us. "This is far beyond what I had expected."

"Couldn't agree more, lad," I mused, grinning with excitement. "Now this. This is what I wanted to see!"

"Sir, as lovely as the entrance is, shall we venture inside?" Wiatt said, letting out a small laugh at my enthusiasm.

I turned to him and my smile grew. "I'm leading the way, Wiatt."

"Right behind you."

The two of us confidently rode up to the gate, eagerly submitted ourselves to their checks and searches; then, once they were done, they let us into the city.

And, once we took our first steps into the city, our jaws dropped.

Directly before us was a great long, central road towards a tall, stone arena which had countless people surrounding it.

Standing along the side of the road as far as the eye could see were hundreds of limestone pillars with carvings of warriors on them, some of which were weathered and damaged, but others that looked like they were carved only yesterday.

To our left were two distinct districts; one was filled with luscious grassland, wooden stalls and hundreds of people, both local and foreign, walking among them, talking happily with one another. The one behind that was filled with limestone and wooden buildings that looked like houses and no doubt served as the place for most people in the city to live.

To our right, however, was a much, much larger district that was so big it could fit the other two districts in it. It was nothing but tall, grand buildings, farms and animal pens. On the streets, we could see Beast Warriors, both on and off duty, as well as many young aspiring trainees of all ages.

I think I spotted a lad of four there following a warrior dressed in a fine boar pelt.

Remarkable.

Truly, Xipe-Totec is a remarkable place.

"Sir?"

"Yes, lad?"

"Where do we even begin?"

We both shared a happy laugh at that and I roughly smacked him on the back. "Wiatt, I think there might be a good place to start."

I pointed straight ahead of us at the arena and Wiatt smiled.

"Aye, sir, that sounds good."

The two of us broke into a sprint down the road; I can only imagine that we looked like excited children to the people of the Narrow, but we didn't care.

If everything that Ikan had told us was right, then that arena would be a place that Beast Warriors would earn their pelts and become protectors of the Narrow.

And those were fights that I wanted to see.

We entered the arena stands and quickly searched for somewhere to sit to no avail. With no other choice, we chose to stand and watched eagerly with the crowd for the trials to begin.

The arena itself was made up of two gigantic stone walls with seats carved into it and at the front was a raised limestone platform which, I assumed, was reserved for the rulers of the city and other people of importance, like the greatest Beast Warriors in Xipe-Totec.

After a few more minutes of waiting, the crowd cheered as a man dressed in fine robes emerged on the limestone platform. He smiled and waved to the crowd before loudly asking them to quieten down.

I don't know what exactly he said but I guessed as much based on how the crowd reacted.

The man then began a long, impassioned speech about…something, not too sure what, and the crowd cheered at certain parts of it, then went as silent as the grave at others. Then, he'd start speaking powerfully again and, for a grand finale, he yelled as loudly as he could and raised his hands into the air.

With a thunderous applause, the robed man stepped down from the platform and others took the seats behind him

Based on what they were wearing, I guessed they were something like royalty here in the city.

A drummer began playing from somewhere out of sight and the first of the hopeful Beast Warriors came out from the gaps at the end of the arena, spear in hand and all but naked aside from a cloth around his waist.

Hang on.
…No.
Surely, they don't…
They don't just kill the dangerous animals alone…but with just that?
…These guys are hardcore.

Four men came out from the side, pulling with them a wooden cage that they dragged with ropes and there was a large and very, *very*, angry boar inside of it.

Its tusks were already red with blood.

The men put the cage in the very centre of the arena; then, without even a moment's hesitation, they pulled open its entrance and ran away as fast as they could. The boar charged out in a fury, squealing, and, I swear to the Gods I'm not lying, the ground cracked from the sheer strength of its hooves.

Even in the face of a beast like that, the hopeful warrior didn't falter.

He lowered his body towards the ground and thrust his spear in front of him; he was waiting for the boar to attack him than dare risk striking first.

The boar saw the man and ran at him at full speed.

It was fast and, if he took that hit straight on, he could end up dead, or very nearly dead at least.

The man thrust his spear towards the boar's face and moved his body to the side, readying to dodge the boar's attack. He missed and it thinly cut at its hide. Just before the boar hit him, he rolled to the side and quickly got back onto his feet, staying crouched low to the ground, his eyes carefully following the boar's every movement.

The boar, too furious to notice its own wound, turned on its heel and charged at the man again.

The man tried the same move again but, this time, the boar ploughed right through the spear, taking the shaft into its side, and smashed into the man's legs, knocking him to the ground. It cried out in pain as the spear splintered against its bones, blood pouring from its wounds, and it struggled to stay standing.

The man, however, looked to be in just as much pain.

From here, I could tell that his left leg was broken and his right had been badly cut by the boar's tusk.

Gods, just looking at him made me hurt; I don't even want to imagine what it must've been like for the lad himself.

He was trying his best not to let the pain show on his face, his lips firmly shut to prevent himself from screaming, but it was obvious just how much pain he was truly in.

The boar turned back to the man and charged once again at him.

Given both their wounds, it would be a struggle just to keep moving, but the man was in a worse situation than the boar.

He didn't have a weapon, but the boar had its tusks.

The man rolled to the side at the last moment, desperately grabbed the broken shaft of the spear, spun around and jumped at the boar. He stabbed it in the back of the head, causing the boar to let out one, final squeal and it collapsed onto its belly. The man fell off the boar onto his legs, which made me wince.

Gods, that must've hurt!

Even with the fight over, the crowd did not cheer.

Just as I was about to ask Wiatt why, the man slowly, and unsteadily, started to stand up. He thrusted one hand high above his head.

He put on the biggest smile that he could and only then did the crowd cheer for him.

And that, I'm guessing, is the end of his trial; the man had won his first pelt.

Wiatt and I joined in with their cheers and claps.

"Sir."

"Yeah, lad?"

"Let's not upset the Beast Warriors even slightly."

"...Yeah."

After that trial, there was another one where a young lad tried his luck against a bear and, against all odds, managed to win, but...well, his strategy wasn't...smart.

I mean, he managed to kill it with only a sharp obsidian dagger, but, once the bear leapt on top of him, I could barely see what was happening.

Well, it worked...whatever he did.

After that, we decided to walk back down the main road and check out the pillars lining it. They were very impressively made with lots of little, intricate details carved into each warrior's armour and weapons; and, if that wasn't impressive enough, every single one that we passed by seemed to be unique.

As we were walking down and looking at them, Wiatt excitedly ran up to one of the pillars and let out a small, excited cry, like a small child seeing a parade for the first time.

I couldn't stop myself from smiling at him when I thought of him like that.

"He your type?" I asked.

"Maybe if he were still alive," Wiatt said back.

We shared a small laugh for a moment; then, I asked, "I take it you recognise this one then?"

"Aye. I can tell by the decorations on his shield."

How in the Depths can Wiatt tell these guys apart?

While I don't doubt that these might have all have their own unique carvings, looking at a few hundred of them back to back made them all blur into one. It was like seeing a hundred men wearing the exact same suits of armour, but they each have different faces, hair styles and colours, and some of their gear is a little more damaged than the others.

Those sorts of minor differences, stuff you could notice on close examination but not from a distance.

"So, who is he?" I asked.

"This is Yochi the Unmoveable," Wiatt said. "One of the Chosen Twelve that stood before Titus when he travelled through the Narrow almost six hundred years ago."

"The Chosen Twelve?"

"Do you not know of them, sir?"

I shook my head. "I thought Titus fought his way through the Narrow."

"Sort of, but not really."

I folded my arms and stared blankly at him.

"...I did it again, didn't I?"

I nodded.

Seems like my message got through to him.

"When Titus came to pass through the Narrow, the representatives of each city gathered to face him with their armies and their Chosen Twelve champions, one for each of the cities. The representatives, not wanting to see their people die for someone else's ambition, offered Titus single combat with each of the champions in exchange for safe passage through the Narrow and an oath that they wouldn't defy him.

"Titus agreed to it and fought all twelve one by one. Each was strong and each fought well, but Titus defeated them all. He could have killed them, but he chose not to as he recognised their strength and agreed with the representatives that dying here wouldn't benefit any of those present. And thus, the Narrow was open to Titus and they submitted themselves to his rule.

"Yochi the Unmoveable was the sixth to stand against Titus. He was legendary among the Narrow because he was never once pushed back in duels with other warriors, until Titus managed it."

"So, he was quite the impressive fella, then?" I asked.

"That's putting it a little lightly," Wiatt mumbled, clearly upset that I wasn't as enthusiastic with Yochi as he was.

I'm sorry about that, but I didn't even know he existed until just now.

"People with titles are rare across the world but, in the Narrow, they hold extra importance," Wiatt continued. "According to Alfyr the Wise's writings, titles are given only to the greatest of warriors every ten years, so having one is one of the highest honours a person from here can have. I imagine that every single one of the people on these pillars had earnt titles in their lifetime."

We moved from that pillar to another one and immediately Wiatt's face lit up again.

"There's another one!" He exclaimed, smiling brightly and pointing at it. "That's Kish Demon's Bane, the first warrior to stand before Titus!"

"Demon's Bane?" I repeated.

"Well, he didn't kill any Demons, but he did kill eight bears in single combat in the arena during his lifetime and barely took a scratch during some of those fights."

"Truly?"

"Truly."

"How in the Depths did Titus beat this guy?" I proclaimed.

"It's simple," Wiatt said. "Kish was good at fighting beasts and monsters, not against people. Titus was the exact opposite and therefore worst opponent Kish could fight." Then, out of nowhere, Wiatt ran up to another pillar. "Xipilli, the Shield of the Narrow!"

I know that a lot of the locals can't understand a word he's saying and yet I felt a bit embarrassed being seen talking to him right now.

Still, I'll bite again and ask.

"Why's he called that?"

"Xipilli was present during an invasion by the Southern Kingdom of the Green into the Narrow," Wiatt began again. "Two thousand Holy Knights and eight thousand men at arms attacked the Narrow, but the Narrow could only muster one thousand five hundred men to defend themselves. Xipilli was leading them and he was responsible for the overwhelming defeat of the Southern forces. Due to his brilliant leadership, the Narrow lost only a few hundred men and the South lost all but a few hundred men, hence why he earnt his name: Shield of the Narrow."

Honestly, when I hear Wiatt talking so passionately about these great warriors who he's never met before and that he doesn't even know if they ever did everything they claimed to have done, I can't help but smile at him.

It really feels like I'm getting to see a very real part of Wiatt that I haven't ever seen before.

"You really admire them, don't ya, lad?"

"Of course I do! Ever since I was a little boy, I'd always wanted to do something great enough with my life that I'd earn a title of my own. After all, it is those with titles and great deeds under their belt that are never truly forgotten, isn't it?"

I smiled weakly. "…Yes, I suppose so."

"I wonder what your title would be if you ever got one." Wiatt thought for a few moments and then said, "How about 'Athellio the Great' or something like-"

"I have one."

"Huh?"

"A title."

Wiatt's expression changed out of the corner of my vision, but I had no idea what it looked like now.

"...Athellio the Wanderer," I mumbled. "Athellio the Wanderer."

"...The Wanderer, sir?" Wiatt meekly asked. I nodded. "How did you-?"

"Because, lad." I turned to him and showed him my pathetic, sad smile. "I can't ever seem to stay in one place for long, no matter how hard I try." I shook my head and said, "It's not a very imposing title, is it?" jokingly to Wiatt.

Wiatt smiled at me. "No, sir. I guess it isn't."

"Well, when we're in the presence of the greatest from the Narrow, it seems even more lame, don't it?"

We both shared an uncomfortable laugh and continued exploring the city in awkward silence, only broken up by forced dialogue between us to try and forget what happened at the pillars.

Typical, ain't it?

I start to enjoy this journey for even a minute and then, in the very next moment, the Gods decide to fuck with me again.

That night, at our tavern, it seemed like Wiatt felt similar to how I did and so proposed that we play a drinking game.

It would, hopefully, allows us to forget the more awkward moments of the day and it could allow us to get to know one another a lot better, so I was very keen to take part in one.

We each ask each other a question and either answered or drunk.

Simple rules, simple to get pissed to.

Easy enough.

"I haven't taken part in a drinking game in ten years," I said.

"Well, sir, let's start of something simple to ease you back into it then, shall we?"

Oi.

Just because it's been a while doesn't mean I've forgotten how to play.

"So, what's your favourite number?" Wiatt asked me.

...I think my jaw might have dropped so far that it hit the table and shattered.

"Sir?"

"How old do you think I am?"

"It's not that, sir! It's just I-"

"Thought that Athellio had forgotten how to play and so I decided to ask him something toddlers ask one another as soon as they learn how to speak?"

"...Perhaps I thought something like that, sir, given your age and all."

"You won't live to see another dawn if you say that again."

We both laughed and then, just to humour him, I decided to answer. "Eleven."

"Eleven?" Wiatt repeated back to me. "Why is that?"

"When I was a kid, there was a bard who came to visit our village every few months, as we lived in a village miles away from all the big cities, meaning some people would spend most of the coin they had just to hear tales from *'far away lands'*." I grunted. "Every time he was in the village, I asked to hear his best stories and he would always tell me his *'Eleven Magic Tales'* each time." I stared off to the side and sighed. "Honestly though, I don't even remember most of them now, not even really their names."

"...It sounds like old age really did hit you harder than I thought, sir."

"I'm not even twenty years older than you."

"True, but you are older than me, sir, and by a fair bit."

I sighed and then asked, "What's yours out of curiosity?"

"That's not how-"

"I know that's not how the game works, but fuck that rule," I said. "If we're going to get to know one another, then we should probably both answer and both drink."

"Alright. I guess that could be fun.," Wiatt replied. He leant back in his chair and then said, "Twenty-two. That's my favourite number."

"Why's that?"

"Because it's how old I am, so my favourite number changes every year."

That...was somehow extremely disappointing to hear.

Gods, maybe I am getting old if just hearing how young he is depresses me.

"Sir, it's your turn to ask a question," he said.

"Oh, right. Uh...um..."

Shit.

I can't think of anything.

Ask anything, Athellio, literally anything, and you'll be fine.

"What's your favourite place that you've ever visited?"

We kept asking each other questions such as this for the next thirty minutes; then, once we were starting to get more comfortable with one another, Wiatt became bolder with his questions.

"Then, it's my turn again. Sir, this might be a bit personal, but I hope you won't mind."

"Ah, don't worry about it," I said dismissively. "Ask away."

"What's the best sex you've ever had?"

If I had been drinking at that moment, I might've choked on it.

"Well, sir?"

I looked him in the eyes, said nothing, grabbed my mug, drunk the entire thing and then slammed it back onto the table, never once breaking eye contact with him.

"Barmaid, can I get another ale please?" I asked.

She nodded, took my mug and quickly ran back to the bar.

"…A strong answer, sir," Wiatt said.

"Your time to answer, lad," I said.

I'm pretty sure I hadn't blinked in at least a minute.

Wiatt grunted, smiled, took a big swig from his mug then, he said, "Every. Single. Time."

I nodded. "Good answer."

We both eventually had to blink and then had a good laugh with one another, just as the barmaid brought me another mug.

"Sir."

"Lad."

"Might I ask another personal question?"

"You might ask one. You might not."

"Sir. I'll be blunt. I'm going to ask you a personal question."

"Fire away, lad."

"What's the worst sex you've ever had?"

I smiled and then laughed a little as I did actually have a good story to answer that.

"This happened just after my fiancé and I had gotten engaged," I said, smiling giddily. "Like most couples, we wanted to celebrate it and wanted it to be an especially special occasion. So, she said that she had this big surprise for me that night and to leave it all to her. But I couldn't do that, so I got some nice smelling candles and flowers together and decorated the bedroom a bit, you know, to help make it more romantic for us both.

"So, that night, I waited with a few low-lit-candles. I was a bit anxious, to be honest, but excited to see what happened next. And then she came in, wearing a gorgeous white dress and my jaw dropped so low to the ground that she almost burst out laughing at my reaction. She slowly walked towards our bed as seductively as she could but, because she'd never done anything like this before." I bit my lip to stop myself from laughing. I quickly calmed myself and continued. "She tried to climb onto the bed, slipped on our sheets, fell on top of me and smashed her knee right into my balls."

Wiatt winced as he let out a small laugh. I chuckled with him.

"Bless her heart, she was so, so sorry and kept apologising to me as I curled up into a ball and groaned," I said. "She also kept asking me if I was alright but I could barely say anything other than a 'Yeah…I'm fine' through gritted teeth. Once I'd recovered, I jokingly said that while we never did it, we did make it memorable and we both just laughed about it."

"That sounds…painful," Wiatt said, still wincing in agony. "Were you fully-?"

"Yep."

"Oh Gods. I'm so sorry."

"Don't be. We made it up to one another a week later."

We shared a small laugh again.

"Aren't you going to ask me, sir?" Wiatt asked.

"I was gonna, but then you said that every time you had sex was your best time, so surely you can't have had a worst time, right?" I remarked.

"Well, you aren't wrong about that. So, it's my turn again then."

"So, it would seem."

I went back to drinking for the time being as Wiatt took a few moments to ponder over what he could ask me.

Given the current flow of the conversation, I imagined that the lad would try to ask me yet another deeply personal question, though I don't know how much more personal you can go with someone than talking about their sex life.

Perhaps it would be something to do with that.

What's the wildest sex I've ever had?

Have we ever had another girl, or guy, with us in the bedroom?

…I wish I had good answers for those.

Gods know I don't.

Now, Wiatt, hit me with everything you got!

"…What's the biggest lie you've ever told someone?" He asked.

His voice had been so soft when he spoke it was almost a whisper, yet I heard that and nothing else in that instant.

That question was more deafening than the dozens of drunken patrons.

"That it's just one more adventure."

I quickly finished my drink, got up and said, "Goodnight, Wiatt."

I didn't even stick around long enough to hear if he had said it back to me.

CHAPTER SIX

My year long trip in the Westerlands really hasn't gone as well as I hoped it would.

After leaving Xipe-Totec, we travelled along the Great Stone Road for four days before we saw our next destination: Itztli: the Home of the Gods.

This was, I am happy to say, one of the cities that I did know existed in the Narrow, but I'd heard all manner of tall tales about this one, before Wiatt dismissed everything that I thought I knew as lies.

An old merchant friend of mine spoke of how he was treated like royalty during his visit to the city.

"A total lie," Wiatt said. "No one, aside from the people from Itztli, is allowed to stay within the city."

I met an adventurer once who said that the priests cast spells of protection on him which, after he left the city, ended up saving his life and him stumbling across a small fortune in a ruin he was exploring.

"I can't comment about that last part, but the Priests of Itztli only ever keep to themselves and rarely speak with anyone but themselves outside of pleasantries, in keeping of their traditions and beliefs."

One bard I met spoke about how the Gods literally walked the streets and mingled with the people, and they were treated as normal citizens by everyone else because, to them, it was normal to have Gods among them.

Wiatt didn't say anything to me and just thinly smiled instead.

I had guessed that this one was a lie, but I still wanted to believe in such a romantic idea.

After Wiatt had quickly shut down almost everything I had heard about the city, he told me about the ritual sacrifices that they performed.

"Once a month, they sacrifice the member of their city closest to death, whether it be due to old age or illness, to their Gods to thank them for their protection and to ask for the deceased to be transported to paradise once their soul arrives in the afterlife."

Then, he told me about two of the most fascinating places in Itztli that we had to see.

"The Great Pyramid sits in the very centre of the city," Wiatt said. "And it stands almost a hundred metres high. From what I've read as well, sir, it's so tall that the pyramid is visible from anywhere within the city, even in the deepest parts of the residents' district.

"The Great Pyramid is dedicated solely to the God Ix-kin Ahu, the God of the Sun and the Moon, and he is said to watch over and protect all the people of the Narrow from atop the pyramid in a palace that we mortals cannot see."

"A protector that controls the Sun and the Moon?" I questioned. "That's quite different from the Church."

In the Church of the Empire, there were multiple Gods for all manner of things, like War, Death, Justice and Love. We didn't have Gods for the Sun or Moon and, if we did, they definitely wouldn't be the ones watching over and protecting Carlen, given everything that's happened lately.

"They say Ix-kin Ahu doesn't just watch over the Sun and the Moon, but all things that are touched by their light," Wiatt continued.

What a truly fascinating prospect that is.

And, excitedly, seeing my face and hearing my enthusiasm for the Narrow, Wiatt continued.

"The Passageway, or the Gateway to the Afterlife," he said. "Is a lake within the city that they dispose of their dead in. Every time someone from the city has passed away or has been sacrificed at the Great Pyramid, their bodies are taken away and all of the flesh is carved off of their bones; then, they take the flesh and pass it into the water of the Passageway."

"…What?"

They carve all the skin…off the bones of the dead…

…Just to throw it into a lake…to what, feed the fish?

"They peel it all off?" I asked; Wiatt nodded. "Every single bit?"

He nodded again. "Well, as much as they can. The people of the Narrow believe that the flesh of our bodies binds our souls to the mortal world and, in order to free them once we have died, they throw the flesh to the creatures of the Passageway to free their souls quicker and to put them closer to the afterlife."

"Because the lake is linked to it, right?"

"Exactly that. According to the tales about the Passageway, at the very bottom of it, is the pathway into the afterlife where you can meet and mingle with the Gods. Or so they say."

"I bet no poor sod's gone to test that out," I grunted.

"I imagine you are right, sir," Wiatt agreed.

"So, what about the bones?"

"Those they bury in a great crypt that they have dug out into the mountain side where all of the dead from Itztli have been stored since the creation of the city. Alfyr the Wise counted as many as he could and apparently found more than half a million skulls before he couldn't keep track of which he had already counted and which he hadn't."

He got that high before he got lost count?

Fucking High Elves have too much time on their hands.

They've got magic, time and talent to do all sorts of things and not worry about wasting it, those lucky immortals.

"Wait, so if they throw human flesh into their only water supply, how do they sustain themselves?" I asked.

"Most of their food gets delivered to them by merchants or traders, either from the other cities of from other parts of Carlen," Wiatt explained. "They do get their water from within the city however, but it's not from the Passageway itself; rather, it is from the rivers leading into the lake."

Well, I'm glad that they don't drink from the potentially tainted water of the lake. After all, if some of that flesh is very disease ridden or particularly rotten when its dumped into the water, I dread to think what might happen to the people who drink from it.

I'm a little bit surprised there are even any fish left in that lake, to be honest.

Maybe it was just the magic of the Narrow?

"I reckon we aren't far from the city now," Wiatt said.

True to his word, just half an hour later, we could see the entrance to the Home of the Gods.

The gate was just as impressive as the one at Xipe-Totec had been, but, unlike that city, this place had walls as well as cliffs protecting it. Strong, limestone walls, maybe five metres tall, ran from the gates and into the mountain side, and nestled into the rockface just before the city walls was a large inn and stables.

"It really doesn't look like a city of priests, does it?" I mused.

"No, sir, no it doesn't," Wiatt agreed. "That over there." He pointed to the inn. "Is the only place travellers are allowed to stay when visiting Itztli."

"Seems a bit mean to force people to sleep outside the walls."

Though, I imagine that inn makes a small fortune every week.

"It's not like they do it because they hate visitors, sir," Wiatt said. "They do have their reasons for it."

"Which are?"

Wiatt opened his mouth to say something, but then immediately closed it and sighed. "I'm not too sure, sir, but it might be because of their religion or traditions." Then, as if hit by a lightning bolt, he sat upright and said, "Although it might be because of something Alfyr the Wise mentioned in his writings of the city. He said that, during the days he visited the city and didn't pray at the Great Pyramid, he felt a powerful shiver and that it was as if someone had wrapped their icy cold arms around him, even when no one else was around."

"Reassuring."

Normally, when most people say stuff like that I'd say they're naïve or misguided, but, when you're a High Elf who can naturally feel magic in the air around you and in the dirt beneath your feet, that's a different story. I'd heard many men from the Westerlands claim such tales before, like the git I met back in the Westerlands who murdered his wife, but they were stories told by people who didn't have the slightest understanding of magic.

High Elves were all born with an aptitude for magic and most of their kind had at least spent a hundred or more years as a scholar at some point in their ridiculously long lives.

Alfyr the Wise was no exception, so it's safe to say I trusted his opinion far more than any humans.

Wiatt smiled in a reassuring way. "On the days he did pray at the temple though, he never felt like that. So, whenever he first entered the city, the first thing he would always make sure to do was visit the Great Pyramid and pray."

"Pray for what?"

Wiatt shrugged. "No idea, sir. He never wrote about his prayers for, and I quote, *'fear of having them not come true'*."

"…Even more reassuring."

I don't know the first thing about the religion that the people in the Narrow believe in, nor do I know what could, or definitely would, upset their God when I prayed to them, so I had to be very, very careful.

"Don't worry, sir," Wiatt said. "I'm sure as long as we don't pray for anything horrible or selfish, we should be fine offering whatever prayers we want to Ix-kin Ahu."

I do hope you're right, my boy. I do hope you're right.

I nodded, then said, "Guess we have our first destination."

Though I said that, technically our first destination was to the inn outside the city to get ourselves a room, then to the stables and then to the city gates; and then to the Great Pyramid.

So, I wasn't wrong in a sense.

The Great Pyramid would absolutely be our first destination once we were inside Itztli.

Once we got to the gates, we were searched and inspected like we had been at Xipe-Totec but this was much quicker and, before we entered, the guard that had examined us blocked our path with his spear.

Confused, we looked to him just as he lent forward and, in a hushed tone, said, "Do not speak too loudly inside the city, for the Gods hear everything that is said within our walls. If you fear their wrath, then speak softly or not at all."

Somewhat taken aback, Wiatt and I looked at each other and then back into the man's eyes; he was not kidding in the slightest. We nodded and bowed to him, not saying a word more to him, and he smiled at us, before bowing back.

Then, in total silence, we took our first steps into the Home of the Gods.

Unlike the other cities before it, Itztli was less built up and clustered than the others had been.

What caught our eyes first, a hundred metres from us, was the Great Temple of Ix-kin Ahu, a magnificent sight to behold, standing tall and strong, made of finely cut limestone, and surrounded by acres of gardens that only royalty would normally ever see.

There was a single stone road leading towards the foot of the temple and, from what I could gather from where we were standing, it looked like it was the only stone road in the city. The two roads beside it leading to the left and right side of the city were made of dirt.

To our right, I could see wooden houses curling along the wall and curving round the mountainside. As there wasn't any obvious market before us, I wondered if it's off to the side somewhere, otherwise how else would people in the city get their food and other necessities.

Perhaps it lay on our left, but I couldn't see from here what was down the left path due to the thick line of trees blocking our view.

Wiatt tapped my shoulder and then put his hands together in a prayer motion, and I got what he was trying to say.

"Priests."

He nodded.

Their district, I guess.

We looked to one another, nodded and began our long walk towards the Great Pyramid hesitantly.

If the Gods truly could hear everything that happened in this city, that meant they could hear our footsteps and, given how a lot of the locals were either wearing sandals or no shoes at all, we both feared that the sound of our boots would upset them.

So, lightly, we trod along the stone road towards the Great Pyramid, matching our speed as best we could to the locals who were walking beside us towards the temple.

As we got closer to the stone steps, Wiatt leant towards me and whispered, "It would appear, sir, that we might have missed the sacrifice for this month."

Towards the very top of the pyramid, we could see a handful of people carrying wet rags, brooms and buckets filled with red water.

Fucking Depths.

I grunted and we both came to the square pavilion before the stone steps where the locals were praying and, somewhat awkwardly, we stood there for a moment and gawked at the size of the Great Pyramid.

I had no idea if it was as tall as what Alfyr had written, but by the Gods I have never seen something like this before in my entire life. I had seen many beautifully constructed buildings in my time, but nothing quite as daunting as this.

It really did feel like I was stood at the feet of the palace of the Gods.

Wiatt tapped me on the shoulder lightly and nodded towards one of the locals who had just arrived at the steps to pray.

First, he bent down to one knee before bending the other one; he then lowered his head, clasped his hands together, then put his hands onto the floor, before lowering his forehead to the ground with his eyes closed.

Before Wiatt moved to do the same, I grabbed his arm and held up one finger, telling him to wait.

Just to be safe, I wanted to make sure that it wasn't just this one local who prayed with such reverence and submission to the Gods, so that we made sure to pray correctly.

Don't want some dark entity clinging to us and bringing death to us now, do we?

After watching four other locals perform the same way, Wiatt and I turned to one another and nodded.

We stepped forward and repeated the prayer movements exactly the same as they did and tried to do it in time with their movements as well.

We bent down onto one knee, then the other, then lowered our heads, clasped our hands together, then onto the floor, and finally lowered our foreheads onto the ground with closed eyes.

I'd never seen people pray to Gods like this before, nor had I ever really done more than a simple prayer of the Church from the Empire, so this was definitely a new, and interesting, experience for me.

Stranger still was when my forehead touched the stone, it felt like I had left the world because everything, and I mean everything, around me went silent.

The birds that had been chirping, the rustle of the locals' clothes as they gently tread around us, the trees and plants that had been flowing in the gentle breeze; all of it went as silent as the grave.

It was only for a moment that we prayed at the steps of the Great Pyramid, but it felt like it lasted for an eternity.

And, in that eternity, I made my prayer to Ix-kin Ahu.

What was it?

…Isn't it obvious?

With my deepest desire conveyed to the Great Pyramid, I slowly got back up, carefully performing the exact same steps as I did, and offered it one last bow that no other local had done.

Just an extra bit of respect for Ix-kin Ahu for listening to my prayer.

Seconds after I was done, Wiatt stood up and we both began to slowly walk away from the temple in dead silence.

Once we were practically right back at the gate, we spoke again and, even then, it was a hushed conversation.

"What now, lad?" I asked.

"Well, sir, it might be best if one of us heads over to the market to resupply our food stores for the next part of the journey," Wiatt said.

"One of us?"

Wiatt tensed a little when I asked that.

...Did he just panic because of that?

"To be honest, I've been feeling a little guilty, sir, since it was my idea originally to rush through the Narrow, even though you wanted to properly see and explore everywhere, so, as we were walking back, I had an idea. What if I went to get the supplies we needed whilst you toured the city and saw everything you wanted to, like the Passageway and the Head Priest's Temple?"

"But then you wouldn't get to see them."

Wiatt smiled sadly and looked at me. "It's okay, sir. I've already had my fill of this city just by seeing one of the Legendary Wonders of the World, so I'm more than satisfied already."

"...You sure?"

"I am."

We stared at each other for a few, uncomfortable seconds, before I exhaled and said, "If you're okay with it, then I'll see you later back here."

"Sounds good, sir. Please, take your time."

And with that Wiatt was off.

So, per his suggestion, I walked around the gardens.

And, yeah, they were beautiful to be sure, filled with exotic plants, trees and birds that I had never seen before, but I wasn't too taken in by them.

Honestly, gardens like these had never been my thing.

Was it pretty? Sure, but I had seen my fair share of gorgeous gardens in my time, including the Rock Gardens, the Cherry Blossom Gardens and the Lily Gardens, the latter of which I definitely didn't sneak into for a few minutes, risking my life by sneaking into the royal gardens of the East.

I had seen all sorts of gardens in my lifetime and these gardens were beautiful, but they were definitely not the best I'd ever seen and, as I'd gotten older, I became less and less interested in them.

Honestly, as strange and potentially boring as this might sound, I was more interested in the priests' living quarters in the city.

Like the inn outside, they were built right into the mountainside itself, not made of stone against it like I'd imagined they would have been, and they reminded me more of tombs than they did places to live.

The priests themselves, based on their calm faces, didn't seem bothered by it.

Perhaps they were like some of the remote monasteries in the Green where they didn't care about physical possessions like everyone else, but instead preferred to live simple, sequestered lives of prayer and devotion.

...I wish I could dedicate myself like that to something.

After walking the full length of the priests' living quarters hoping to see anything else, I gave up, turned towards my right and walked for just a few moments before I spotted the other landmark Wiatt had told me about.

The Passageway, eh?

It certainly didn't look like one, no matter how you sliced it, and it definitely didn't look like the gateway to the afterlife.

Its water was a clear blue and sparkling brightly in the sun, filled with fish and other creatures living within it, and even the rocks decorating the edges were gorgeous in their own right.

How could something so picturesque have such a horrific practice attached to it?

The more I gazed at it, the more confused I became.

I mean, it was beautiful; truly, amazingly, beautiful.

So beautiful in fact that I wanted to jump into it right there and then, armour on and all, and bathe in its waters.

It smelled divine and the waters sounded like they were still, even with all the fish swimming around in it.

...Wait, that wasn't it; the water was moving and fish were swimming in it, yet it didn't make a single noise.

How strange.

Then again, almost everything that I had seen in the Narrow thus far was strange. I mean, I saw a man kill a bear by letting it jump on top of him and spent time among a city of only farmers.

This, strangely, felt mild in comparison, almost like...it wasn't even that weird.

Wait, why did I think it was weird to begin with?

...There's nothing wrong with this lake.

Even its smell, despite the amount of human flesh dropped into it, smelt fantastic-

...It doesn't smell anymore...

How...nice...

I wonder how refreshing it would be...to swim in that water...

Perhaps I should...I feel like I need to cool off...

I mean...I can barely see anything anymore...must be the heat getting...to me...

...Must be...

...

Can't...think...anymore...

...I need...to...
Hydrate...
...and fast...
Before I...pass out...
A small dip...wouldn't hurt...
Of course it won't...
Why would it-?
Ah! A blinding light?!
"The fuck?" I cried.
Gods, it's so bright!
"What the Depths?"

I covered my eyes and averted my gaze; I'd never seen the sun shine so brightly off water in my entire life.

"Oh no."

Oh no, oh no, oh no.

I didn't want to think of what had just happened so, being the sensible man that I am, I walked as swiftly as I could away from the lake, not daring to look back and ignoring the few, dwindling voices in my head telling me to go back and swim in that water.

Gods know what would've happened if I'd-

...The God of the Sun and the Moon?

I turned to the Great Pyramid, then slightly behind me, not too far though for fear of looking upon the lake again, then back to the pyramid.

Surely not, right?

Best not mention this to Wiatt.

Don't want to scare the lad or worse make him want to go and see for himself.

Well, after that, I met back up with Wiatt by the gates and was happy to see that he had bought enough supplies for us to last for a fortnight at least.

"Good work, laddie," I said, showing him a not forced, happy smile. "How much I owe for my share?"

"Don't worry about it, sir," he said, handing me a sack filled with my share of the supplies. "I'm more than happy to cover it with my own coin, as you'll be paying for drinks for us at the next inn."

"...Did I say that?"

"You didn't." He grinned at me. "But I thought you might."

I let out a sigh and shook my head a little. "You cheeky bastard." I smacked his head lightly. "You got yourself a deal."

"So, did you find anything else worth seeing in the city, sir?"

...

"Sir?"

"...Nah," I said with a dismissive wave. "It's all pretty much just gardens and priest buildings over there."

"Did you not find the Passageway?"

"…It was closed for the time being…due to them…disposing of human flesh."

Slightly disappointed and confused, Wiatt hung his head a little and mumbled, "I see."

Lad, I don't like lying in general, especially not to you, but this is for your own good.

With nothing else to do in the city and evening quickly reaching us, Wiatt and I went outside the city to the inn that had burrowed into the cliffside and had dinner, before being shown to our beds.

Not rooms, beds.

Not even beds, really.

Stone holes in the side of the rocks that we could crawl into legs first and feel warm from midnight to morning, or at least that's what the locals said.

We stored our supplies in our horses' packs, bid each other a goodnight after a couple of drinks, and crawled into our stone holes.

The owners gave us soft duck feather pillows to rest our heads on and, to their credit, the stone beds were extremely warm, but not uncomfortably so, so I couldn't really complain about our sleeping arrangements, especially when it was the only inn for travellers to stay in that didn't cost a fortune.

I was never exactly comfortable with small, cramped places, but I was strangely relaxed and feeling quite good as I was drifting off to sleep.

Maybe that's a part of this city's magic, or maybe I was blessed by Ix-kin Ahu.

Whatever the reason, I'm grateful for it.

CHAPTER SEVEN

From the moment I opened my eyes, I knew I had to be dreaming.

After all, rather than seeing the rock ceiling of my bed, I saw a stone house in the middle of a field with a woman sat outside of it.

It was the house I had bought with all the money that I had saved up over my years adventuring, back when I actually made money from my adventures.

However, it wasn't as I remember seeing it just before I left for the Westerlands.

It looked exactly like it did nine years ago, back when we had first gotten engaged.

And Sarah was smiling happily at me.

"I still can't believe you're going," Sarah said.

"Why wouldn't I?" I sat down beside her. "What adventurer worth a damn wouldn't want to see the beauties of the far eastern kingdom? The Lotus Gardens? Root Town with the last of the Great Sakura Trees in it? The Jade Palace and its collection of art that dates back before the Dread Dawn? What could be more wonderful than seeing those?"

Sarah pouted a little. "I can think of something better."

"As can I, but." I smiled. "I wouldn't be able to settle down without seeing the east. I know I wouldn't."

"Why wouldn't you?"

"Because that was the place that first inspired me to be an adventurer, all those years ago," I said. "When I was six, a visiting bard told a grand tale one night about the Great Sakura Tree and how beautifully it bloomed all year long. He described it as if it was the most beautiful thing in the entire world and that captivated me. Whenever I would see the trees around my home, I wondered how much prettier the Sakura Tree was, how much taller it was, just how old it was…how something like that was one of the few things to survive through the Dread Dawn."

After that, we were silent for almost a minute.

Sarah interlocked her fingers with mine.

"You promise this will be your last adventure?" She asked me.

"I promise," I said, smiling. "I just want to make sure I've seen everything worth seeing in the Green before I settle down for good. I won't be gone for more than a year and then, once I'm back, we'll have the rest of our lives together."

Sarah smiled at me and we kissed.

"I can't wait!" She excitedly said.

Just after I had turned thirty and I was looking back on my life, I wondered when I first wanted to be an adventurer and I realised that it had been because of that story.

Not some grand tale of fighting a dragon, not one of saving the world from danger, and not one of rescuing the princess.

It had been to see a single tree.

When I had first started travelling around the Green, I had intended to go north first, then make my way west and travel around the entirety of Carlen, making the east my final stop and, at that time, I had fully intended to do so.

But then, when I was in the city of Lotus where the Great Sakura Tree was located, I desired to see the Eastern Province and so, being the young, naïve adventurer I was, I got on a boat that same day, thinking of how great it'd be to end my journey when I got back to Carlen by seeing the Great Sakura Tree.

I thought, in a way, it would be a poetic ending to my own adventures that bards might speak of one day.

However, I was drawn to another adventure and then another and then another, and, before I knew it, I had met Sarah, gotten engaged, and then still found myself travelling around the world even after seeing the Great Sakura Tree.

It was just as divine and beautiful as the bard had described, but a thought had surfaced in my mind when I saw it.

What other beautiful, wonderful things were there in this world like this that I hadn't seen?

And so, I travelled again and again in search of more adventures and more wonders.

I scowled as the dream around me began to fade.

I thought that I had been given some sort of blessing by the Gods but, instead, I got a cruel reminder of the old days, when Sarah still saw me off with a smile.

…Honestly, when was the last time I saw her look at me that happily?

***

When I awoke, I pushed everything that I had seen and felt in that dream deep down inside me and got ready to set off.

***

After we set off, Wiatt and I continued on along the road for four days before we arrived at the next city: Atlacoya, the Dry City.

This was one that I was very familiar with and it was one that was well known across all of Carlen, though many dismissed it as a romantic idea conjured up by bards and adventurers in a futile attempt to wow people.

And, like them, I thought that the city was made up.

Apparently, in Atlacoya, people didn't need to eat food to stave off hunger, nor did they need to drink water or ale to quench their thirst. Nor were there any rivers or lakes within the city. The craters where they had once existed were dry and barren.

So then, how did people manage to live in and survive in the city?

Simple: the magic of Atlacoya kept them alive.

So long as one stayed within the boundaries of the city, you never needed to eat or drink to survive and could live a long, healthy and happy life without ever having to worry about two of the most basic needs to stay alive.

Quite the fairy tale, eh?

To be perfectly honest, I didn't believe it existed either until we got to the city.

Once we had reached the gates and were being checked by the guards, they asked us for our food and drinks, offering us a stone chest adorned with strange markings to place them in. I had wanted to object, understandably so, but then I saw a group of people near us placing their supplies in them as if it were the most natural thing to do.

"Sir, if the stories are true, then it shouldn't be an issue," Wiatt said to me in a hushed voice.

"Agreed, but that's a big if, lad," I mumbled.

Still, it was pretty obvious from the way that the guards were acting that we wouldn't be allowed entry into the city if we didn't hand over our food and water.

Begrudgingly, we did so and were permitted entry to the city.

Now, to be perfectly clear, when I had first heard about Atlacoya when I was a young lad, I had been a bit of a religious boy, believing in the glorious Heaven above us forged by Titus after his death and that in his *Kingdom of the Clouds* we could live in peace for eternity, never needing to eat, sleep or drink.

When I had first heard of Atlacoya, I was seven years old and my mind raced with ideas about what the city could look like.

I imagined walls made of pure white stone with gilded patterns, marble paving spreading for miles and miles without end, with beautiful gardens and oases filled with divine smelling flowers too beautiful to describe with the words of mortals.

Perhaps, I wondered, if Atlacoya was Heaven on Carlen made for mortals.

Well, reality is a bitch.

Inside the walls of Atlacoya was something that looked more like a ruin than a city.

Dried, cracked land and rocks decorated the ground. In the empty holes where there had once been rivers and lakes were the buildings of the city, nestled against the banks. Depths, even the gates we had entered into the city from were connected to one of the dried-up rivers and there were armed guards protecting the staircases up and out of the trenches we found ourselves in.

The buildings were not made of marble or gold, nor were they a pure white. They were a dull, muddy brown with cracks in them, and old wooden supports to keep them standing.

Truth be told, I was a bit disappointed in what I saw, especially when I compared it not just with the image I had of it in my mind, but also how all of the other cities we had visited looked.

"So, sir, shall we get exploring?" Wiatt cheerfully asked, though he was not as enthusiastic as normal.

I nodded and we decided to spend most of the day exploring the city, hoping to find something of note worth seeing or investigating, but, alas, we found nothing.

It was just a regular, plain city with none of the charm of the rest of the Narrow.

With that said, by the time the sun started to set, and we had to begin searching for an inn to stay at, Wiatt and I both looked at one another and asked practically the same thing.

"Are you hungry?"

"Are you thirsty?"

Despite being on our feet all day and doing nothing but walking, we didn't feel like we had to eat or drink anything, not even a little bit.

Huh, I guess the stories about Atlacoya might have some truth to them after all.

We found an inn close to the gates, rested and, when we woke in the morning, neither of us felt any different.

Normally, when you wake up, you'd want something to eat or drink, so not having that feeling was bizarre.

It was very strange.

But, unfortunately, there was no reason for us to stay in the city any longer so we promptly left and reclaimed our supplies. They had been left untouched in the chest and they handed them back to us before we had even given our names to them. Then, we rode off towards the next city: Ehecatl.

It wasn't until the next morning that we felt hunger and thirst again.

I think I've begun to understand why people would be so willing to stay in such a remote city like Atlacoya now.

Though, I can't help but feel like something is lost when you don't need to eat or drink, like it's something that makes us alive so, if we were to lose that, then it's almost like we're undead now.

Wiatt and I made sure to eat a slightly bigger breakfast than normal just in case before setting off on the road again and, after just three more days riding, we were pretty close to Ehecatl: the City of Storms.

It didn't take long for me to see how it earnt its name.

Out of nowhere, the sky above us became greyer and, ahead of us along the Great Stone Road, we could see rain and lightning relentlessly attacking the mountainside in a terrifying display of Mother Nature's power. The thunder roared at us like a lion, warning us of its strength and that to get too close to it was the same as asking for death.

"Damn, I guess we were too late in getting here," Wiatt lamented, sighing and rubbing his brow. "I'm sorry, sir, but we won't be getting to Ehecatl any time soon."

"Why? Surely, we just have to wait for the storm to-" Before I even finished my sentence, I cut myself off and lowered my head. "Lad, I think I know, but explain why we can't get to Ehecatl soon?"

"The City of Storms has always been beset by terrible and powerful storms during this time of the year, ever since the city was built. The storms, like that one we can see, can last for days, maybe even weeks, on end without relief. The longest recorded storm in Ehecatl's history was almost two months long, I believe."

"Fuck, really?! That long?"

Wiatt nodded. "I had hoped we'd be fast enough to avoid it." He turned away from me and clicked his tongue. "Shit."

...

I think that might be the first time I've ever heard Wiatt swear or, at the very least, with such ferocity.

"So, lad, what do we do? Wait it out?" I asked. "Maybe find a village nearby to stay in for a while, or head back to-?"

"We can't!" Wiatt yelled, spinning to glare at me, scaring the shit out of me. He quickly composed himself and said, "Sorry, sir. I didn't mean to yell."

I smiled reassuringly at him. "It's fine. I'm just as annoyed." I surveyed our surroundings and saw several dirt paths split off from the Great Stone Road, and I pointed at one that seemed to lead us down more towards the coast. "Why don't we try that path?"

Wiatt spun to look where I was pointing and thought it over. "That might work, but it could end up taking us right into the heart of the storm if we aren't careful."

"...I mean, as long as we keep an eye on it, I don't think it'll sneak up on us."

Wiatt laughed at that and said, "The lightning bolts from the clouds can shoot as far as a mile from the edge of the storms of Ehecatl. See that there, sir." He pointed to a very blackened piece of ground that I had somehow managed to miss by the side of the road. "That was where one struck, quite recently too as well from the looks of things."

I didn't say anything to that.

Though, I did ride my horse forward a few paces before stopping right next to Wiatt.

"So, shall we give it a go then?"

Wiatt nodded.

"Then, let's get going before we lose more daylight."

We continued riding again along the dirt path. We prayed that it would lead us down to the coast, a good distance away from the storm, and then we'd loop back up to the Great Stone Road much further along, far away from the raging storm.

Alas, this time, we would not get to see Ehecatl in all its glory.

As we were riding, my mind was filled with questions that, annoyingly, I wouldn't get answers to in a long, long time.

How did the city's buildings not get destroyed by the storms every time they came?

What was it like to be within a city during a storm that lasted for days on end?

How could they sleep in peace, or do anything without the storm disturbing them?

Could they grow crops or fish safely within the city itself, or did they have to gather those from outside the city and risk being caught off-guard by a sudden storm?

Well, all these questions I'd have to hang onto until the next time I came to visit the Narrow.

A shame, without a doubt, but at least now I had something to definitively achieve when I came back to the Narrow.

But, even though we were missing out on the city, we were much safer travelling down this path than we were taking the Great Stone Road at least.

***

If I ever get the chance, I'm going to kill all the fucking Gods in the world.

"Afternoon, fine gentlemen," a man with very few teeth and a drawn sword said to us as he emerged from the bushes. "Dangerous to travel round these parts."

Whenever I think I'm having a good day, those damned deities must cackle and giggle to themselves before thrusting shit like this my way.

Toothless here and four of his friends surrounded us, on foot, two with swords, one with a spear and two with one handed axes. They weren't in proper armour but they definitely had a fair number of scars on their faces and limbs.

…Fuck the Gods.

Fuck 'em.

Wordlessly, we stared at them for a few moments, neither Wiatt nor I moving for our weapons, as we both assessed the situation.

I imagine, based on their lack of muscles and proper form, that these men weren't trained warriors, but common cutthroats that preyed on villagers and caravans without guards, or maybe they were refugees who had managed to sneak out of the Westerlands, or just common bandits.

Whatever the reason, I couldn't care less.

They dared to threaten my life and that was enough for me to want to kill them.

"What can we do for you men?" Wiatt asked with his usual bright smile on his face.

I could tell that he was faking it. They, somehow, could not.

Toothless let out a small laugh and said, "We don't 'ave time to waste on chatting, not with the storm raging up 'ere. So, 'ere's the deal. Give us ya valuables, or die. Simple as."

Well, at least he wasn't wasting our time.

It meant we'd get to kill him sooner.

Wiatt, still smiling, got off his horse and didn't take his sword as he did, and slowly moved towards Toothless. The bandits raised their weapons and I dropped my hands to my side, preparing myself to leap off my horse at one of the bandits with an axe.

If Wiatt is who I think he is, he can hold his own in a fight.

I already had my dagger strapped in its sheath at my thigh, and I could definitely kill the bandit without my sword, so it was just a matter of timing.

I'd strike when Wiatt did.

Toothless moved right in front of Wiatt and the two stood staring at each other for a small eternity, neither moving, Wiatt still smiling, and Toothless still aiming his sword at Wiatt's chest.

"Ya want to die?" Toothless barked.

Wiatt slowly, and purposefully, shook his head from side to side. "No. Do you?"

Furious, Toothless stabbed at Wiatt, but Wiatt used the back of his arm to knock the flat part of the blade upwards, making the strike miss. Wiatt then kicked Toothless hard in the shin, dropping him down onto one knee, before kicking him in the chest.

The bandits were, for a second, too stunned to move and I struck right there and then.

I leapt off my horse, drew my dagger and ran up to the bandit with the axe. He swung at me, so I dodged it, then grabbed his wrist and stabbed him in the heart.

I removed my dagger and the bandit fell down dead.

I grabbed his axe and threw it towards the one with the spear, catching the man in the thigh, causing him to scream wildly in pain.

I saw Wiatt run back to his horse and draw his sword, just before the other bandit charged at him. Wiatt blocked his first few swings, then beautifully parried one and sliced the man's stomach open.

The other bandit with an axe ran at me, swinging madly. His attacks were slow and easy enough to dodge, so all I had to do was wait for the best time to strike. He swung wide and I stabbed him in the throat, killing him instantly.

I turned to Wiatt just to see him get struck in the back by the bandit I had seen him strike down.

"Wiatt!" I screamed, rushing towards them.

Wiatt howled in pain, kicked behind him, pushing the bandit back, spun around and cut the man's head off. Toothless went to stab Wiatt in the back, but I stabbed him in the stomach and then threw him to the ground.

The last living bandit, the one with the spear, tried to limp away, no doubt hoping to escape, but I wasn't going to let that happen.

I picked up the other axe and threw it at him. It landed in the square of his back and the man fell flat on his face dead.

After that, I quickly went to check that the other bandits I had fought were dead.

I wasn't going to let us get sneak attacked again.

I sheathed my dagger and ran to Wiatt. He was on his hands and knees, breathing heavily.

"Wiatt!" I crouched beside him and could see blood trickling through his shirt. "Fuck! I'll bandage you up, just give me a sec!"

"I'll...manage, sir..." Wiatt said through gritted teeth. "It's...not as bad...as it looks."

"The fuck are you on about?" I grabbed the bandages and herbs from my pack and ran to his side. "Get your shirt off so I can-"

"No!"

I jumped back and was left speechless.

That shout was louder than the one he had made when he been sliced by that bandit.

...Why?

Seeing the confusion in my eyes, Wiatt's expression became even more pained than it already was, and he turned to face the ground. "As long as you don't...look at my stomach...please..."

I nodded and went behind Wiatt.

I took off his chest piece, then lifted up his shirt as Wiatt held it down at the front and began tending to the wound.

Thankfully, it wasn't deep.

His armour had taken most of the impact, but it had still gotten through and cut the skin, albeit quite lightly.

I cleaned the wound with water from my waterskin, then applied herbs to it and then began bandaging it, passing them forwards to Wiatt to help me pass it across his chest. After two minutes, his wounds were patched and I helped him sit up right against a nearby tree.

"How's the pain?" I asked.

"...Better," he muttered with a thin smile. "Still hurts like a bitch though."

I smiled. "Do you want to set up camp here and rest for the night?"

He shook his head. "Can't risk it. The storm could...grow...and hit us."

"Then, we should get moving soon. If these guys were here, then there's a good chance that there's a village nearby."

"How do you figure?"

"It's simple, really. Bandits hit often travelled roads, so there must be somewhere nearby that travellers rest in, a village I reckon."

"...Sir, if you don't mind...could you help me up onto my horse?"

I smiled weakly at him. "Just this once, lad."

I slowly helped him up onto his feet, then carefully got him back onto his horse, and we continued onwards. I had tried to insist that we move slower so we didn't upset his wound, but Wiatt was very adamant that we keep to our original pace.

I don't know why but within the space of a few hours I feel like I've seen a side to Wiatt that he wanted to keep hidden from me.

We were on the road for three hours before we came across a fishing village, just as the sun was beginning to set. We inquired with a local herbalist who spoke Carlian if there was somewhere that we could stay, but they told us that there were no inns in the village.

"I could try asking the villagers, but they might not want foreigners staying with..." The herbalist trailed off as he was staring at Wiatt whose face I'd only just realised was much paler than normal. "Is your friend sick?"

"We were attacked by bandits on the road and he was wounded in the fight," I explained. "I treated his wounds as best I could, but I guess that it wasn't enough."

"If it is alright with you, I could take a look at it and give you shelter for the night."

"I thought you said the villagers didn't trust foreigners," Wiatt said.

The herbalist smiled sadly. "They don't, nor do I. But I cannot leave an injured person untreated before me."

"...Then, we'll take you up on your invitation," Wiatt said.

We followed the man to his home where he showed Wiatt to one room and then asked me to stay in another, so that I could go to sleep first whilst he tended to Wiatt's wounds. I had wanted to protest initially, but then I remembered how Wiatt had acted before about his stomach when I had tried to treat his wounds on the road.

"Make sure he's okay," I said, before closing the door to my room.

I changed out of my gear, lay down on the bed and stared blankly up at the ceiling for ten minutes before I even felt remotely tired.

My mind was busy processing everything that had happened today.

The great storms I'd seen, the bandits we'd fought and whose lives we'd taken, and the thing that stuck with me the most: how Wiatt acted when I tried to tend to his wounds.

I'd never heard him lash out like that and it scared me.

Then, just as I felt myself about to drift off to sleep, I heard someone shouting.

It was loud, very loud, but I couldn't tell who it was that had been shouting. The walls were thicker than I had thought, so it was impossible to tell, though I could guess who.

After that, there was nothing.

I waited for a few minutes, my hand reflexively reaching for my sword, before I heard the herbalist say, "Good night and I hope you feel better in the morning," to Wiatt and retire to his own room.

Whatever had just happened, Wiatt was alright for now.

CHAPTER EIGHT

Neither of us spoke about what had happened the previous day for the rest of our journey to Tlaloc.

Just before I asked Wiatt if he was feeling better, he immediately started talking about stuff we passed like normal, and I found myself caught up in his rhythm.

We kept talking like that for a while until we could hear the very feint sounds of music coming over the hill, causing Wiatt to smile.

"We must be quite close to Tlaloc, sir," Wiatt said.

I shot him a quizzical look. "How can you tell?"

"Tlaloc is called the City of Thunder and Lightning, but, unlike Ehecatl, this city got its name because it is always loud and always bright in the city. No matter what day of the week it is, and no matter what time of the year it is, there always seem to be a never-ending party happening all year round in Tlaloc."

"Truly?"

"Truly. In Alfyr's writings, he noted that Tlaloc was the only city that he spent two months at and, in that time, he said there were twelve festivals in those months."

"Fucking Depths!"

That many in just two months?

"Alfyr left after fearing how many they might have in a year and that he wouldn't be able to handle the noise," Wiatt said.

"How much does that cost them to do?" I blurted out.

Wiatt shrugged. "Not enough that it's a concern for them."

I whistled loudly and Wiatt let out a small laugh.

In Wheatcraft, we had village wide parties for some people's birthdays, like the mayor, and we celebrated weddings and the like, but those were uncommon events, once in a year sort of things.

"How many things can there be to celebrate in a year?"

"I don't know but, from what I remember reading, they seemed to have a festival for everything you could think of."

"Like what?"

"Rain, Sun, Fire, Earth, Air, Creation, Fertility, Hunting, one for each of their Gods, Hunters, Warriors, Priests, Marriage, Dea-"

"Okay, I think I get the idea."

Wiatt smiled and I let out a small sigh.

How can they have that many festivals within a year and still function as a city?

That said, if they really did have that many festivals and parties across the year, then perhaps, like Wiatt had said, we'd stumble upon one.

It'd make for a good change of pace, given everything that's happened.

Especially in the last city.

"Still, sir, we personally do have something to celebrate, don't we?" He asked, smiling brightly. "We can celebrate surviving a bandit attack, can't we?"

"Aye, I'll drink to that!" I bellowed.

Just as we agreed to that, the gates of the city came into view.

Before we were allowed to enter the city, we had to hand over our weapons and place them in similar boxes to those we saw in Atlacoya.

Once we were in Tlaloc, we did our normal routine: find an inn, store our belongings securely in our rooms, tend to our horses and then get exploring; except, this time, we didn't have to go far to find what we were looking for.

As we stepped out onto the street, the crowd cheered as a massive parade began its march along the road.

When we had originally entered the city, the music we had heard on the road had died down, so we were worried that we might've missed the festivities, but it seemed like they were only just getting started.

The people in the parade were dressed in all manner of clothing. Some had vibrant headdresses made of brightly coloured flowers, others were wearing animals skins akin to those we had seen from the Beast Warriors of Xipe-Totec, a few didn't have anything more than a fur pelt at their waist on them, showing off their beautiful tattoos on their skin, and most of them were wearing jewellery of some kind, whether it be as obvious as a bracelet or as subtle as an earring.

Those in beast pelts were carrying animal skin drums and banging on them in almost perfect synchronisation. Those with their tattoos on display were dancing with ribbons and long wooden sticks, flicking them up into the air fashioning patterns as they did so. A couple of them had guitars that they were playing as they ran and danced, and others carried flags bearing golden animals on white cloth.

The crowd excitedly cheered for them, with many of them clapping or dancing along to the music as the parade went on. Wiatt and I quickly found ourselves caught up in the atmosphere of the city and joined in.

The parade continued like this for a long time until, all of a sudden, everything went quiet and the musicians stepped to the side, allowing the dancers to take centre stage along the road. What followed was a dance and song routine so gorgeous that words honestly fail me.

I was so absorbed in their performance someone could've robbed me blind.

Though maybe I could feel that way because the guards didn't allow anyone else in the city to carry weapons.

After a few minutes, the performers stopped and it felt like the whole city cheered for them.

Naturally, we did too.

The whole parade continued like that for hours on end. The musicians would play, then a dance and song would happen, and so on and so on.

My personal favourite moment of the night was a staged sword fight that two men and a woman were doing along the main street. It was an intricate, beautiful flurry of clashes and attacks, resulting in one of the men being *'killed'* when he was *'stabbed in the heart'*. While I couldn't understand what they were singing, the crowd seemed to love the story that was told in that dance and cheered loudly once it had concluded.

We joined in with them.

By the time the parade had ended, the sun had set and the city was lit up by candles, lamps, magic stones and runes, along with strange, luminous plants that I had never seen before. The street was getting livelier and more crowded than when the parade had come through, so Wiatt and I decided to go back to our inn for the night and we were in high spirits.

Even in the tavern, it was overflowing with people, ale and merry laughter. It was quite an infectious mood which then quickly enveloped us as well.

We ordered a few drinks each, sat at a table towards one side of the room and began to drink like there was no tomorrow.

Pint after pint, ale after different ale, contest after contest, we drunk and talked and played games with one another.

We raced each other to see who could drink their pint the fastest, escalating the strength of the ale as the night went on. We placed bets on who in the tavern would pass out from drinking too much and, towards the twilight hours, we challenged one another to perform silly acts in front of everyone.

I challenged Wiatt to jump onto our table and to dance and sing as loudly as he could, which he did and the entire tavern even joined in with him.

It seemed that a good number of people in the city spoke Carlian, a very pleasant surprise, but I could guess why. If I knew that there was a city that always partied this hard and with this much merriment, I'd want to see and experience it for myself.

After Wiatt did that, he leapt off the table and then challenged me to tell my best, and worst, jokes to the crowd. I finished my pint, said, "Fucking gladly, mate!", stood up, and yelled at the top of my voice my funny joke.

Though, I don't remember what I said or did, but people seemed to laugh and I almost collapsed after I'd done it.

I was starting to feel a bit queasy and it was getting harder and harder to keep my thoughts straight.

"Looks like you need some water, sir," Wiatt said before burping loudly. "Here, have this."

He pushed towards me a cup of sparkling blue water which I was too intoxicated to question and drunk from it. Like magic, my mind began to clear up and my urge to throw up vanished completely.

"What was that stuff?" I asked Wiatt.

"Pure Water, I think the barmaid called it," he said. "Said they have wells in this city that purify the effects of drinking too much ale, which is why they can keep drinking and partying like this." Wiatt then took a mug filled with the same liquid and drank it. "Gods, that does make you feel a thousand times better, don't it?"

"Aye, it does. Lad, I forgot to ask, you don't know what kind of festival this one's meant to be, do you?"

"I asked the barmaid, sir, and she said it's a fertility festival today."

"Well, that certainly explains a lot."

Perhaps not about the parade itself, but the way the people were acting in the tavern. There were lots of men and women sitting together very intimately and many were either heading upstairs or outside for some *time together*. There were also plenty of lonely men and women looking for partners as well, such as the three beautiful women staring at our table, smiling and giggling at us.

Wiatt turned to see what I was looking at, turned back to me and grinned, and then asked, "Sir, are those girls your type?"

"If you mean beautiful, then yeah, I guess," I said. I waved at the girls and they slowly began making their way towards us.

"Sir, I know this isn't a drinking game, but which of those women do you want?"

Before I could answer, two of the girls wrapped themselves around me and one sat on Wiatt's lap, lightly pecking his cheek.

He blinked rapidly a few times and coughed a little, no doubt taken aback by how much her breath stank. After all, these girls were no doubt very drunk like we had been. Or, at the very least, had been drinking a lot and then taken the Pure Water to clear their heads a bit, like we had.

I smiled smugly and thought to myself that our shenanigans earlier must've caught their eye.

"Lad, I think this answer your question," I said, standing up and escorting the two ladies with me.

"It does, indeed, sir!" Wiatt called to me as he got more...acquainted with the women on his lap.

I took the fine women up to my room and they quickly begun to undress me. I held their lower backs and pressed them up against me, making them laugh a little as they got my armour off.

Gods, when was the last time I was ever with a woman, huh?

Probably not since-

Sarah-!

Just before the women could remove my shirt, I let go of them and asked them to stop.

"What's wrong?" One asked me.

"I-I...I'm sorry, but I can't do this..." I said, taking a step back. "...I have a fiancé. I'm sorry."

The two women looked at me, then each other and nodded. They said they understood and left my room.

Once they had gone, I waited for a few seconds, then locked the door and pushed my back against it, letting out a long and weary sigh.

"...Honestly, what the fuck am I doing?"

I poured myself a glass of water from the jug the barmaid had brought up when we'd arrived and then walked out to the balcony, sitting on one of the stone chairs and gazing up at the stars.

It was, quite honestly, difficult to see them inside Tlaloc because of the amount of light coming from the city, but a few of the stronger and bolder stars broke through nonetheless, as did the moon.

Somehow, when I looked up to them and could barely make them out, I felt incredibly upset and like I was a thousand thousand miles away from where I wanted to be.

Here I was, at long last, in the mythical land of the Narrow, a place I'd longed to see since I was a wee lad and all I could think to myself was how quickly I wanted to be done with this place.

It was gorgeous, wonderous, magical and oh so beautiful to see such legendary places and know that they exist, but, right now, as I was surrounded by cheer and happiness, I felt depressed.

I brought my forehead to my hands and sighed once again.

How much longer can I really keep living like this?

If I had made one wrong move the other day against those bandits, I'd be dead.

If I had been dragged into the Passageway back in Itztli, Gods know what would've happened to me.

Depths, even before that, back when I was adventuring around the Westerlands alone, how many times did I come close to death?

How many times should my life have been taken from me before that? I chuckled bitterly at myself.

It was honestly a miracle that Sarah was even still my fiancé after everything that has happened.

Over the years, she would see me off and each time she became less and less attached to me, treating it as something that didn't concern her anymore.

It went from her saying it sadly and sweetly, to worried, to concerned, to unfazed, and to uncaring after that.

This time when I had left, all she had said when I had gone was this.

Bye.

Bye: with the coldest, most painful to gaze upon eyes I had ever seen in my life.

I had stared death in the face, seen bandits and monsters up close that threatened to take my life, but those eyes…Sarah's eyes…were the only ones that truly haunted and lingered with me.

I threw myself onto the bed and wanted to curl up into a ball, my mind filled with an image of that scene replaying endlessly.

"…I miss you," I whispered, my eyes beginning to water as I hugged one of my pillows tightly.

CHAPTER NINE

For once, I got a rough night's sleep in an inn that wasn't caused by alcohol.

I let out a heavy sigh, had a glass of water, and cleaned myself up as best I could before going to the balcony. From what I could tell, it seemed to still be pretty early in the morning based on how low the sun was.

In the streets below, I could see the people beginning to clean up the mess left in the streets from yesterday's events. Though, strangely enough, I thought I could see people setting up for the next parade.

Gods, don't these people ever get bored of parties?

I took a deep breath, exhaled, smiled, put my boots on and went downstairs.

Given how early it was, I imagined I had woken up before Wiatt had. After all, unlike me, he had been drinking for a lot longer than I had been and no doubt he was still in bed, with a massive headache, wondering what the fuck he did last night.

"Morning, sir!" Wiatt cheerfully greeted me.

Downstairs, at the bar, with an empty plate and a mug of water, was Wiatt, his normal bright smile on his lips and no signs that he had been drinking heavily the night before.

Lucky bastard, having that much alcohol and not even being a little hurt in the morning.

Must've had a lot of that *'Pure Water'*.

"How was your evening?" He asked me.

Shit, he's expecting me to tell him of my great night that definitely did not happen.

"…Yeah, it was great…How was yours?"

He beamed even brighter. "It was terrific, sir! I had seven pints of their specialist ale, slept with a beautiful woman and, best of all, when I woke up, I remembered every little bit of it. I don't know how it would compare to your evening with those two but, this woman, Gods she was good."

For the sake of my own sanity, I decided to block out all the details that Wiatt proceeded to tell me about his more intimate time.

"Anyway!" I interjected before he told me about their second round. "I need to get some food and drink myself."

"Ah, sorry, sir; I didn't mean to-"

"Don't worry about it," I said, smiling. "I'm happy to hear you enjoyed Tlaloc this much."

"It wasn't just Tlaloc I-"

"Are you sure you don't need a bit more sleep?"

He shook his head. "I'm perfectly fine, sir." He then got off his seat and said, "I'll pack my things and get the horses ready."

"Thank you. I'll try not to be too long."

I ordered some breakfast, had another glass of water, packed my stuff and went out to the stables where Wiatt was already waiting, both horses untied and the reins in his hands.

We left through the city gates and continued along our journey down the Great Stone Road.

Though, we didn't stick to it for very long.

About three hours after we'd left the city, Wiatt started taking us down a dirt road that seemed to lead closer to the coast than it did the next city: Chantico, the City Built from Ash.

It was a city that I was quite interested in seeing, as it was the only one in the Narrow to have been built after the Dread Dawn following the destruction of the city Xolotl by a volcanic eruption.

However, when I pointed out to Wiatt that Chantico was in the opposite direction to where we were heading, he said, "I'm sorry, sir, but I didn't think you'd want to see it."

"Why wouldn't I?"

"Well, truth be told, it's quite the dull place according-"

"To Alfyr's writings, I know, I know. So, we're cutting it out and just heading straight to Atlaua?"

"Actually, I wanted to visit another one first."

I instinctively frowned. "Where?"

Wiatt turned to me, smiled and, without a hint of sarcasm or deceit, said, "Xolotl."

Xolotl, the Burnt City, the City of Ash.

The city that the Demons had destroyed more than a thousand years ago.

During the Dread Dawn, the Demons launched attacks across the world to try and destroy all peoples and civilisations with their armies and magic, the latter of which they used to cause natural disasters.

Like, say, a volcanic eruption that spewed molten lava and fire for miles around, unleashing a gigantic cloud of ash and dust over the nearby city of

Xolotl. The gases, ash and dust blanketed the city, killing all who lived inside, turning them into Ash Men and Women, fearsome monsters who killed all that entered the ruins of the city.

To this day, fires still rage inside Xolotl that had, according to legend, been burning brightly and strongly since the city fell. The air is so thick with ash that it is difficult to breathe and see within the city.

From what I've heard of those foolish enough to get close to the city and make it back alive, just taking a small breath is enough to make your lungs feel like they're on fire. Some say that those who died in the city have their souls trapped there for all eternity, only able to escape by dragging a living person's soul in to take their place.

Put simply, why the fuck would anyone ever want to go near such a place except to go there, see that the stories are true, say, "I like living," and go back to the main road and carry on your damn way?

Wiatt, please tell me that's why you want to go there.

Please, please, please!

"Why?"

"Why?"

"Yeah. Why?"

Wiatt smiled. "Doesn't it sound exciting, sir? Venturing into a ruined city, fighting an Ash Man, discovering a long, lost treasure or relic that was thought destroyed? Surely that has to be exciting to an adventurer like you, no?"

"What the fuck is exciting about certain death?" I spat back. "You go near the city; you choke. You go into the city; you get lost and either starve or dehydrate. You stumble across an Ash Man; he burns you alive until there's nothing but a charred corpse left. What's exciting about that?"

Wiatt frowned. "Where's your sense of adventure, Athellio? I mean, surely, you'd want to see something like Xolotl, right? Even if it's from a glance?"

"Lad, if I've learnt anything from our trip through the Narrow, it's that myths, legends and stories about this place have been true a lot of the time, and I have no reason to doubt Xolotl will be any different. So, why take the chance, even if they are wrong?"

"Because we won't get another chance in our lifetime to see this place, will we?"

"And I hope I never see such a place."

Wiatt stopped his horse, turned to face me, still scowling, and folded his arms. "Not even a glance from a distance? Not even just to see something as haunting as this?"

I laughed in disbelief. "Why would I want to see something as horrific as Xolotl? Why? So I can get haunted by the souls of the dead? Or killed by a man made of ash?"

"Gods be damned, why not? Just for five minutes? You wouldn't even have to go into the city."

"I wasn't planning on even if you dragged me-!"

Wait.

"What do you mean by that?" I asked.

"What do you mean, what do I mean?" He asked back.

I scowled and bellowed, "What do you mean *I* wouldn't have to go into Xolotl?"

"Well, since we've come all this way, I plan on at least exploring a bit of the city."

"You what?!"

"I plan on exploring the-"

"Do you want to die?"

"I want to live."

"Then-!"

"I want to live a little for once in my fucking life and have a real adventure!"

I was taken aback.

That wasn't just an angry shout like the times Wiatt had yelled at me before.

...This...was coming from somewhere else...

"What's wrong with having a little thrill, huh? Don't adventurers and travellers risk their lives for the sake of experiencing something great and exciting, even if there's a chance they'll die? Depths, that's why some men sign up to join armies! Athellio, with or without you, I am going to Xolotl and going into that city."

What are you, eight?

Or a particularly annoying lover?

"Then fucking go on your own!" I shouted. "You're an adult, right? Then fucking go on your own for all I care. See if I care if you get killed by Ash Men or burnt by fires, or choke on ash, or-"

"Will do then! See you at Atlaua!"

...He actually rode off to Xolotl...

On his own.

After throwing a tantrum.

...Did this just happen?

Before the realisation of what had happened fully hit me, Wiatt was out of my line of sight.

Huh.

I mean, it's probably fine, right?

To let him go off by himself, right?

I mean, this is just like before at Atlacoya when he did the shopping on his own.

...except there's smoke so thick that you can't see what's right in front of your face...

...and the air's meant to be toxic to breathe in if you take too much into your lungs...

...and there are fires that have been burning for more than a thousand years...

...and monsters that will burn him alive...

...He'll be fine, right?

Like I said, he's an adult.

He can handle himself...

...alone, in the city that personifies death...

...with a wounded back-

What the fuck am I doing?!

I kicked my horse into action and rode as hard as I could towards Xolotl.

Wiatt, even if I have to drag you out of there myself, I'm getting you out of there!

You damned fool!

I'll fucking break your arm when I find you!

If you're coming back towards me though after chickening out of going into the city, then I'll settle for snapping off one of your fingers for making me worry so much.

Where is that damn-?

Wait, there's his horse!

I rode over to it and found it lashed to a tree, maybe a dozen metres walk away from the smoke that covered the city.

Up close, I could tell that it really was just as thick and foul smelling as the stories told. I couldn't see more than ten feet into the city itself and I could only make out vague images of stone walls and pillars.

Without a torch, it'd be impossible to see anything in there.

Thankfully, being the overprepared and cautious adventurer I am, I had torches in one of my packs. I took one out and lit it. Then, I packed another into a pack I'd take with me into the city and slowly made my way towards the smoke.

Admittedly, I didn't know if Wiatt had truly entered Xolotl, but I didn't imagine he would've turned tail and run after coming so far.

Of course not.

Despite how calm and polite he seems normally, he can be reckless like he was the other day and even long before that. After all, it takes balls to try and leave a nation under lockdown like we did.

I did it out of desperation; I still don't know why Wiatt did.

Before I fully stepped into the smoke, I wet a piece of cloth and tied it around my face so that it covered my mouth and nose.

If the stories about the smell and thickness of the smoke were true, then

I had good reason to believe that the molten gases and eternal fires were real as well.

Even from here, it felt like the air was tougher to breathe and I wondered if I was taking ash into my lungs.

I treaded cautiously into the city and my eyes were snapping from one place to another constantly, scanning for Wiatt or for the Ash Men and Women that roamed the streets.

I walked for two minutes into Xolotl down a central street that in its prime might have led to the city square, but the stones that it had once been made of were now soft ash that threatened to drown my feet if I wasn't careful with how lightly I stepped. Before me, maybe ten metres ahead, I saw the first of the eternal fires.

And it was burning brightly and unlike any other flame I had seen.

It was a deep red with licks of black flames rising into it. It was as tall and wide as a carriage and it was emitting a scorching heat that made my skin crawl and sweat.

From what I knew of the Dread Dawn, when the Demons had attacked, they unleashed all manner of powerful spells and attacks, some of which were as powerful as natural disasters and whose effects were felt for all eternity.

The old Nordic continent of Aage was destroyed by earthquakes and tsunamis and, if the legends are to be believed, the Demons caused them. Xolotl was destroyed by a volcanic eruption the Demons unleashed and it buried the city in ash, lava and molten rocks.

If that was true, then these flames had been burning for more than a thousand years.

I walked around the flames and hoped that I would spot Wiatt as I did, or that he would see me and call out to me, but all I found was rubble, ash and the bones of those foolish enough to come to the city before me.

How did I know?

Because there was still charred flesh on their bones.

"Ash Men," I whispered.

I looked to my left and thought I saw something moving in the smoke.

I froze.

Slowly, I reached for my sword, pointing my torch towards the thing I'd seen, or that I thought I'd seen, and held my breath.

My ears pricked up and I waited, listening for any sounds.

I couldn't hear anything other than the beating of my heart in my chest and the hiss of the eternal fire behind me.

I stood there for about a minute before I dared to move again.

It would seem like my eyes were playing tricks on me.

Still, caution is always advisable, especially right fucking now, so I moved even more carefully than I had before.

Then, I realised something that, honestly, I should have realised sooner, but I had been too focused on finding Wiatt to properly pay attention.

Which way had I come in?

The only landmark that I had was the eternal fire and, for all I knew, there were plenty of identical ones like that within the city. Perhaps the Gods would smile on me and a very powerful wind would blow through Xolotl, clearing the smoke away and allowing us to find each other and get out of here.

If Wiatt's even still alive.

…I hope those bones weren't his.

If an Ash Man catches you, then there's nothing you can do.

You can stab them, beat them, kick them and beg them to spare you, but they will still incinerate you all the same.

Perhaps caution and sneaking around wasn't the best option.

I was confident in my stamina, but I don't think Wiatt could say the same. His wounds hadn't properly healed and Gods forbid he's unable to move without splitting his back open.

I picked up my pace and continued down the street.

As I did, I notice that it became clearer to see my surroundings, though I didn't know if that was because my eyes were adjusting to what I was seeing or if, like I had hoped, a strong wind had cleared some of the smoke out of the city.

Gods, please let it be the latter!

As I searched, I didn't find anything new or different than what I had already seen.

Rubble.

Bones.

Fires.

Depths, for all I knew, I was walking around in circles.

I cursed under my breath and started-

A stone was kicked behind me.

Slowly, Athellio.

…Slowly…

Ash Men react to movement.

Slowly turn.

Slowly check.

Gods, let it be Wiatt…

Of course, the Gods aren't that kind…

Just metres behind me, shambling down the road I had just walked, was a man who looked like he was made of stone, stone as white as the clouds in the sky.

His body was stiff and refused to move and bend like it should.

It was emitting deep voiced groans and moans that croaked, like he was sick and his throat was dry.

It turned to look at me and I felt the blood rush from my body.

Its eyes burnt like a furnace.

A flame, just like the eternal fires, was burning in those otherwise empty sockets, its throat was black and dark ash was falling from its gaping mouth.

This...

This is how I die.

...Sorry, Sarah...I won't be coming hom-

It titled its head, confused, and gurgled.

What's it doing?

Still, I dare not move, not when it's looking right at me.

It turned and...

...walked away?

Slowly, it shuffled away from me, back into the smoke and vanished right before my eyes.

...How am I not dead?

Aren't the Ash Men ruthless monsters that kill all living things on sight?

They burn people to death, right?

Like that poor sod I saw before?

Right?

Right?!

Hahahaha!

I really wanted to start laughing and cry out to the heavens in joy, but I keep it muffled and settled for a hushed giggle instead.

A joyful giggle!

My knees gave out.

Tears fell from my eyes.

I'm alive...

I'm fucking alive!

Wiatt!

I shook my head, dried my tears and got back to searching for my companion.

While that Ash Man spared me, there's absolutely no guarantee that it would spare Wiatt or that Wiatt was even still alive.

Maybe the Ash Man had spared me because it already eaten and had its full for now with Wiatt's flesh. Well, if it needs to eat, that is.

Gods I hope not.

Though, there must be some reason as to why the Ash Man decided to spare me.

Perhaps...no, I mean, maybe...maybe the Ash Men aren't aggressive-

No, that doesn't work. I saw those charred bones myself, so there is definitely something in Xolotl that is burning people alive but it might just not be the Ash Men.

I really, really don't want to imagine what other horrific beasts lurk within this city.

I have to find Wiatt and soon!

I sped up my pace and began searching everywhere I went, high and low, behind walls and rocks, and by any eternal flames that I saw. Thankfully, I didn't run into another Ash Man as I searched, but I always kept my eyes and ears open just in case one appeared.

Just because I got lucky with one once, doesn't mean I'll get lucky with it again.

Perhaps I should start calling Wiatt's name, but that could bring something else with it.

Shit!

"Wiatt," I said in a soft voice. Then, a bit louder, "Wiatt."

Nothing.

"...Sir?"

Please tell me that's not a very polite monster!

Please, tell me that's not a very polite monster!

I turned and saw, close to the eternal flame I had just walked past, was Wiatt, without a torch and covered from head to toe in ash. He also didn't have cloth over his mouth and nose, even though I'd told him about the gases.

"There you are!" I was about to shout, but quickly got control of my voice and managed to keep my voice low as I spoke. "You alright?"

He laughed and rubbed his head in embarrassment. "My torch went out when I tripped over. That big fire's the first light I've seen since."

I let out a long sigh and forced myself to smile. "If you're okay, then that's what matters. Still, we got to go and now. The Ash Men are real."

Wiatt's eyes widened. "Truly?" I nodded. "You saw one? How close?"

"Face to face. Didn't attack though, don't know why."

"Hmm. Were they-?"

"Worse than the stories. Now, come lad, let's-"

Thud.

Thud.

Thud.

Those...were footsteps.

...Footsteps as heavy as a brick smashed against the ground.

"Sir, is-?"

I raised a finger to my lips, then grabbed his arm. I pulled him behind a wall I could see and we hid up against it.

Confused, Wiatt went to look out from behind our cover, but I held him back.

I then plunged my torch into the ash beneath us, extinguishing the flame and I refused to move an inch.

Thud.

Thud.

Something growled, but its voice was not that of an animal or a man. It was like a furnace, roaring after fuel was thrown into it.

"I thought you said the Ash Man didn't attack you," Wiatt whispered.

"I did. But that isn't an Ash Man."

"How do you-?"

I put a finger to my lips again and slowly looked around the corner of the wall.

Thud.

Thud.

Whatever it was, it was getting closer and closer.

I could see the eternal flame and another faint red glow, but it was a decent distance from us.

As long as the smoke remained, I wouldn't be able to see its source.

I hid behind the wall, turned to Wiatt and then mimed to him that we needed to slowly move away from here. I then quietly started walking away from whatever that light was.

While I didn't know if the Ash Men could see or not, I did know that they were slow moving, at least, as long as we were quiet, so I had hoped that we could escape whatever that monster was under the cover of the smoke.

Slowly, one foot after the other...like a babe learning to walk.

Careful, Wiatt.

Try to watch where you step.

Try not to step on anything but ash and dirt.

We can do this-

Wait! The air just changed!

Oh no.

No, no, no, no!

Not now!

Not a fucking strong wind now!

It was strong enough that my hair whipped against my eyes and my sword in its hilt began to move with the wind.

"Sir."

"...Yeah, I know."

We quickened our pace but, right before our eyes, the smoke was starting to clear and we could see things further and further away from us.

We could see everything five metres from us.

Then, in the next moment, ten metres.

Then, twenty.

Then, thirty.

Then-

Thud.

The monster growled.

We stopped dead in our tracks.

We turned slowly around and saw it.

A creature the size of a human made of ash as dark as obsidian with furnaces of bright red flames in its eyes and mouths. Unlike the other Ash Man I had seen, this one's body seemed to move more like a human's, but it also had claw like fingers which had recently dried blood on them.

It cocked its head when it saw us.

Then, with another mighty thud, it stepped closer towards us and growled.

It was staring right into my eyes.

This wasn't a man made of ash, but a woman.

If the Ash Men didn't kill those who came into this city, did the Ash Women do it?

Is that the only misconception people have about this city?

If I wasn't looking right at this monster, I swear I would laugh.

It felt like I was staring into the eyes of death itself.

The Ash Woman straightened her back, then moved its body like it had just taken a deep breath, before screeching in a voice louder and more piercing than the most furious banshee.

"Run!" I yelled.

We both broke into a sprint and the creature ran right after us.

I looked back over my shoulder for just a second and saw that it was much, much faster than we were.

I clicked my tongue, grabbed Wiatt's arm and dragged him down a side alley just as the Ash Woman leapt towards us.

It smashed into the ground where we had been standing and the impact knocked the ash around us up about a metre into the air.

It howled and followed us down the alleyway.

At that moment, I had a flash of inspiration and wanted to test my theory.

"In there!" I cried, pointing to the ruins ahead of us.

I don't know if Wiatt got my intention, but he followed my lead.

We ducked into the ruined archway and, as we did, I hid behind the wall and yanked Wiatt to me. As I had done that, the Ash Woman had jumped at us again and flew through the ruins into a wall.

"Yes!" I screamed, dragging Wiatt out of the house and we continued running.

"Sir, did you know it would miss?"

"Yeah! We can do this if we can keep this up!"

Just as I had hoped, the Ash Woman, despite its great strength and speed, wasn't a creature driven by intelligence or a desire to hunt.

It was only driven by anger and that we could exploit.

If we couldn't beat its speed and we couldn't fight it, then we could out manoeuvre it and, given by the smile Wiatt was making, he knew what I intended to do.

The Ash Woman came running out of the house, roared at us, and then began the chase again.

Even though we had been running for a few seconds more, it still caught up to us in no time at all.

So, the idea was that every time it got close to us and went to attack us, we would duck behind cover or into a house, trying to time it as best we could to when it was leaping at us, and then keep running but in a different direction.

As long as we could get out of the city limits, we'd be fine.

Well, I hope we will.

I'd heard stories from the few survivors saying that the Ash Men didn't pursue people who had left Xolotl so, if that was true, all we'd have to do is escape the city limits and we'd be fine.

Even if they'd gotten the damn gender wrong, I prayed that this bit wasn't wrong.

Shit, here she comes!

I ducked behind a large rock and Wiatt did the same.

The Ash Woman landed before skidding along the ground a few metres away from us. It lost control of its landed and rolled over, but immediately snapped back up onto its legs a second later.

"That way!"

Wiatt nodded and we made a run to our east but, as we got going, I noticed that Wiatt was moving much slower than he had been just a few moments ago. His face was slightly pale and he looked like he was in great pain.

Did he hurt himself when-?

Shit!

His back.

Wiatt's wound probably reopened during all the commotion, so of course he can't run like he did before.

There had to be something, anything, I could do to help him, right?

If I slowed down to help him, we'd both be caught by the Ash Woman and die.

If I told him to take off his gear and leave it behind, it could take too long.

Could I try and fight her and buy him time?

Even if I could, fuck that.

I'm not dying here and neither is he!

"Sir!"

Wiatt tackled me to the ground just as the Ash Woman leapt over us and smashed onto the ground, tumbling and turning again and again.

"Thanks, lad," I said, quickly getting us back on our feet.

I hastily surveyed the area around us and saw a long street to our right which had lots of buildings, rocks and ruins for us to hide behind.

Perfect.

"Over there, now!" I shouted.

"Yes, sir!"

We ran for it and the Ash Woman pursued us.

And got ready to do as we had done before…except she didn't fall for it.

We ducked behind a rock, but the Ash Woman howled and smashed her foot into the rock, reducing it to tiny pieces, a few of which hit us.

Fuck!

So much for that lack of intelligence!

The Ash Woman then brought her foot down towards us, but we leapt forwards, narrowly avoiding her kick which left a crater in the ground.

We ran and ducked behind cover again and, just as she had done before, she destroyed our cover and went in for another attack. Wiatt got up onto his feet as the Ash Woman jumped at us. We barely dodged it in time and kept running.

"Sir, it's not much further!" He cried.

"How the fuck do you-?" I started to ask, until I could see exactly what he meant.

I could see our horses.

"Run faster than a fucking stallion!"

Wiatt inadvertently let out a low chuckle as we ran.

The Ash Woman was so close to us now that I swear I could feel her breath on my neck.

It was disgusting, like being right next to a furnace in a blacksmith's, just as hot and just as fowl smelling.

I shivered, drew my sword and turned to slice at her, but the Ash Woman stopped running as I did. I struggled to keep my balance and almost fell over due to the sudden momentum shift of my body, but Wiatt supported me, letting out a loud yell as he did.

It seemed like he was approaching his limit with his back.

We kept running and running and running, neither of us turning around again for an instant.

We weaved our way through rocks and ruins, rubble and buildings, through the main street and the side streets, almost being caught by the Ash Woman again and again, barely escaping our death.

Just ten more metres to go!

Come on!

The Ash Woman stopped growling and I heard a fire ignite behind us-

Gods no!

No, no, no, no, no!

No!

"Down!"

I jumped belly first onto the ground and Wiatt did so just a split second later.

As he did, a roaring black fire flew over our heads, as hot as the eternal flames in the city, but it stopped after just a few seconds.

I spun onto my back, sword in hand, and blocked the Ash Woman as she jumped on top of me.

She grabbed my sword and began tightening her grip on the steel.

The blade began to creak and break under her strength.

I couldn't shake her off, nor could I let go of the blade.

If I did, then she'd be able to kill me.

Depths, even if I didn't, she'd be able to kill me in just a few seconds.

Wiatt swung at her with his sword and I half expected it to shatter once it hit her.

Instead, there was a bright white spark and the Ash Woman shrieked, leaping away a dozen feet. She roared and stomped her feet hard, cracking the ground around her as Wiatt stood between me and her.

I didn't know what exactly had happened, but it seemed like she was scared of him.

"Get the horses!" Wiatt cried, taking a far swing at the Ash Woman, spooking her.

I didn't even pause before running to my stead.

I cut the ropes binding her to the tree, quickly flung myself onto the saddle and galloped towards Wiatt and the Ash Woman.

Just in time, too.

The Ash Woman ran at Wiatt and ducked under his swing, then grabbed him by the throat, dragging him against the wall. She roared in his face, spitting black ash all over him.

As I rode towards them, Wiatt slashed at her again with his sword, making her scream and retreat again and, a second later, he took my arm and climbed onto my horse. I rode into the city, turned back on myself down a side street and galloped out of the city limits before the Ash Woman could catch up to us.

She pursued us right to the edge of the city and stopped.

She roared at us once more, spitting more blackened flames, but didn't make a move on us, even though it would be easy for her to charge and kill us right there and then.

But she didn't.

Not as I rode back to Wiatt's horse, nor after we both collapsed off of mine, both exhausted from our time in Xolotl.

By the time I could bring myself to look at the city, the Ash Woman was already gone.

I let out a sigh of relief and lightly hit my head against the dirt.

We were alive.

Behind me, I heard Wiatt start to laugh as he shifted onto his back, staring right up at the sky.

"Well, that was quite the ordeal, wasn't it, sir?" He mused, laughing and smiling like an idiot. "That right there is an encounter few others could have said to have been through and survived, so I imagine it'll make quite-"

I punched him right in the cheek before he could say another word.

I punched him fucking hard.

"Sir-?"

I hit him again, jumping onto his front.

I was grinding my teeth together and my body was shaking from top to bottom.

I hit him just as hard again on his other cheek.

Then again.

And once more on the other one.

I stopped myself when Wiatt spat blood to one side, his face already beginning to change its colour.

"You reckless fool!" I hit the ground next to his face. "Why did you do it?! You're young, got your whole life ahead of you, so why, why would you throw it away like-?"

...like I would...

When I was his age, I had done things just as reckless and stupid as he had just done, throwing caution far beyond the wind and venturing into the heart of danger just for the thrill of it.

Back when I first started out as an adventurer, I didn't think about what would happen tomorrow or the day after; I just wanted to find an adventure just like those I had always loved bards telling around campfires. I wanted to go on an adventure like the heroes of old, finding ancient treasures in ruins, through myself into the most dangerous situations imaginable and come out of them alive and forging myself as a true legend.

I've done that for almost twenty years now, ever since I left home at eighteen.

What right did I have to criticise Wiatt for it when I would do it too?

Did I not learn every time Sarah looked at me with those eyes that were filled with a deep sadness that threatened to consume me every time I looked into them?

I slipped off Wiatt, fell onto my back and stared up at the sky, staring blankly at it.

"Sir?" He asked.

"...Fuck," I mumbled, closing my eyes before tears poured from them. I put my arm over them and sobbed. "Fuck."

I couldn't see Wiatt's face but I could imagine just how confused he looked but, right now, I didn't care.

I was just relieved that I was alive and heartbroken about how great a fool I was.

CHAPTER TEN

I refused to speak with Wiatt for days after that.

He, on the other hand, kept speaking at me as if nothing had happened and apologising every so often for being reckless.

"Lovely weather we're having today, isn't it, sir?"

"Oh! Would you look at that. Isn't that a Golden Falcon? I've never seen such a beautiful bird before in my entire life."

"My wounds seem to be a lot better today, sir. Much better, in fact. Perhaps they're starting to heal properly."

"My back doesn't hurt anymore, sir."

"Thank you, Athellio…for saving my life in Xolotl. If it hadn't been for your bravery and kindness that day, I would be dead."

For days, he would keep talking to me and I would never say a word back to him, even when he told me about the next city in the Narrow.

"Atlaua: the City of Fishermen," Wiatt began. "Apparently, the name came not just from the amount of fish that they eat, but because of the ridiculous number of fish living in the city itself. The lake and the rivers in Atlaua cover more than half of the city itself and there are supposedly tens of thousands of fish living in them.

"The residents don't just catch the fish within their waters however. They also have several small villages along the southern coast less than a mile from the gates where they fish for even more food." He chuckled. "Believe it or not, sir, they have to trade for other goods quite often, like vegetables and cattle, as all they can really sustain themselves with is fish. They don't have enough room or grasslands to farm themselves, so they have no choice but to import it. Unimaginable, isn't it?"

Gods, Wiatt, what the fuck is wrong with you?

One minute, you're like this, the next you're a mindless fool who doesn't value his own life.

Even after we fought and even after everything we went through, how in the Depths can you continue on as if nothing had ever happened?

During the fourth day of my silent treatment, I finally decided to respond to him again.

"In Alfyr's writings, he spoke of great wild birds in Atlaua like eagles and falcons that lived in the city and were so intelligent that they could walk on two feet beside the residents as if it was the most natural thing in the world," he said. "I'd love to see such animals if they exist, wouldn't you?"

"...Yes, that does sound amazing," I said softly.

Hey, what can I say?

I'm still pissed with him, but I don't hate the boy and want to stay his friend. It's just that I wanted him to understand the seriousness of what he had done.

I wasn't even looking at the kid and I could tell his face lit up brighter than the sun.

We arrived at the city soon afterwards and, when we went inside, we were greeted by a crisp breeze and the smell that was just like that of the sea.

At the very heart of the city, as Wiatt had described, was the great lake of Atlaua: Lake Chiccan.

It was a beautiful, deep sapphire blue. Resting on its surface were dozens of wooden boats manned by fishermen and flying high above it were hundreds of exotic birds, many of which I had never seen before.

Before us was a steep stone ramp that lead into the city itself and, branching off it were dozens of cramped alleyways and roads overflowing with people. Walking among the people we could see animals of all sizes and species walking along with them, not afraid or scared, but bravely and intelligently, almost as if they were human.

"You'd think the Narrow wouldn't surprise me anymore," I mumbled too quietly for Wiatt to hear.

We just stood there, mouths agape and clueless, standing at the entrance as crowd after crowd moved around us.

If there was ever a time when we looked out of place in the Narrow, it was at this very moment.

We both looked at each other and then walked over to one side of the road, pushing ourselves as far out of the way as possible along the main road and stood there in silence for a few minutes.

...This was awkward.

Very, uncomfortably awkward.

"Is there anything in particular you want to see, sir?" Wiatt asked.

I shook my head. "...What's worth seeing?"

I think Wiatt looked very upset when I asked him that.

I guess he had told me more about this city than I remember and I had forgotten all of it during my *Ignore Wiatt* phase.

"Well, there's Lake Chiccan," Wiatt began. "In their tongue, it means *Paradise of Nature*. Um, there's also *The Spider*.*"* I glanced at him. "It's a group of five rivers on the east side, but located behind that is a great tomb where all of the dead of Atlaua are buried. According to Alfyr, it got its name from the fact that their dead are buried in a network of tunnels they call *The Threads*' and they spread for miles into the mountain side."

That doesn't sound creepy or horrifying at all.
And after what happened in Itztli I don't want to take any chances with a place like that.
"On the other side of the lake is *The Behemoth's Claw*'," Wiatt continued. "It's a group of four rivers that look like a gigantic claw. According to the local myths and legends, during a great war between the Gods of the Narrow, a mighty beast known as the Behemoth appeared and fought in that war. It was said to be such a powerful and ferocious beast that was strong enough to carve away the toughest mountains and those rivers are a result of one such attack."
I grunted and said, "That would be pretty terrifying if that was the case."
"I think so, too," Wiatt said.
"...When's that war meant to have happened? Before the Dread Dawn?"
"Alfyr's writings didn't tell me much, I'm afraid. He got inconsistent reports from the locals, with some saying before the Dread Dawn, some after and some even said it took place tens of thousands of years ago in the Lost Ages. No one knows, sir, though some say that the Behemoth was a powerful Demon and not a monster from the Gods."
Still, whenever it was meant to have happened, I had to admit, I was very interested to find out the rest of the story about this *War of the Gods*'.
It sounds like it would be a fantastic tale, one of the great legends of the world, and, even more excitingly than that, it was one that I had little information about, meaning it would be a new story to experience.
Maybe I could find someone to ask about it, or perhaps a book merchant and ask if they have it.
I needed to find out.
"...Where do you want to go, sir?" Wiatt asked.
"I want to see the Behemoth's Claw and then see if I can find a book merchant. What about yourself?"
"Personally, I am more interested in seeing the Spider and the tombs buried there."
...Yep, it's awkward again.
For the first time since we'd been in the Narrow, we didn't want to see the same places.
But maybe it was for the best that we were going to spend our day away

from one another, give us time to clear our heads and deal with our feelings.

Yeah, maybe that'd be for the best.

"Sounds good," I said. "So, shall we go find an inn for the night?"

Wiatt smiled. "Sounds good."

So, we did just that.

We spent about ten minutes getting rooms for ourselves at an inn near the gates, put our horses in the stables and set out on our own paths through the city.

Though, unfortunately, as I quickly found out, actually navigating through this city was very difficult.

It was filled with thin, steep, narrow pathways and staircases, and there were so many people moving along them that I had to stop and wait for others to pass before I could go any further. It also didn't help that there were so many animals walking around as well that I had to keep an eye out for, as I didn't want to injure them and I didn't want to upset the locals by hurting them, which would then resulting in them hurting me.

I had to pass over many bridges as well to get close to the Claw.

From the entrance, it had looked like no more than a thirty-minute walk to the Behemoth's Claw, but it took me about twice as long to reach it.

There were, as I had expected, very few buildings around it and those that were there looked abandoned long ago, though I had no idea what the reason could be.

The terrain in this part of the city was quite rough and difficult to walk on, let alone build houses on, but it was doable, the empty buildings next to me proved just as much.

Still, as a result, this part of the city was far more beautiful to me than the rest of the city. It was filled with gorgeous plants and flowers, and there were all sorts of wildlife living near the Claw, from cats and dogs, to large birds of prey and cattle.

One bird in particular caught my interest.

It was a gigantic bird with golden feathers, a black beak and large wings nestled against its back. It was perched on top of a sharp rock and turned to face me. Its eyes were a deep shade of brown and it titled its head at me.

I smiled at it and sat down on a smooth stone that I saw.

From here, I think I could see the entire city and yet I could barely hear the noise coming from the other side of the lake.

Here, at the Behemoth's Claw, it was just me, the animals and a spectacular view.

It was so relaxing and peaceful.

It makes such a nice change of pace, you know, from almost being burnt alive by a woman made of ash a few days before.

Atlaua, you're a beautiful place.

A black and white cat lightly jogged towards me and leapt up onto my lap, catching me by surprise. It curled up into a ball and stared up at me.

I smiled and began stroking it. It purred happily and shut its eyes, rubbing itself against my legs.

"Cheeky little bastard, ain't ya?" I whispered.

The cat meowed happily.

...Did it just understand what I said?

Wiatt had mentioned that the animals in the city were very intelligent and very friendly, but I hadn't expected this.

The cat hadn't gone for the food I'd brought with me in my pouch or anything; it had just jumped up eagerly onto my lap and only wanted somewhere to rest and to be stroked.

I looked back up from the cat and saw the gigantic bird from before slowly walking towards me, looking curiously at my face.

"Hello there," I said, waving at it with my free hand. The bird bowed to me. "Would you like something to eat?"

The bird bowed again.

Was that its way of nodding?

I reached into my pack and pulled out two pieces of meat, one I put on my lap near the cat in case it wanted something to snack on and the other I offered to the bird. It quickly moved to eat it right from my hand and, to show its thanks, it brushed its face up against my cheek.

I stroked its head and couldn't stop myself from grinning like an idiot.

This.

Was.

Great!

Its feathers were not only the most beautiful I'd ever seen, but they were super soft as well!

I wish I could take you home with me!

I wonder how much meat I'd need for that?

If taking this bird back would be too difficult, then maybe this cat would be a better option?

The bird was gigantic and, after I'd fed it, it had spread its wings for me and it had a wingspan of about thirteen feet. So, getting home would with it would be difficult.

Well, in that case, I best spend as much time as I had with these animals before I had to leave then!

Well, I love animals, so, right now, this is probably my happiest moment of the last year!

***

After spending perhaps a little bit too much time talking to and playing with the animals, I decided to head back towards the inn we'd be staying in because of how late it'd become.

I mean, I have no idea where the Depths Wiatt was, whether he was still at the Spider's Web, or if he'd gone somewhere else.

And searching for him in a city this big with this many pathways and alleyways was out of the question, I thought it best to just head to the inn instead.

Atlaua's beautiful, it's amazing, it's filled with fantastic wildlife, and it's a gigantic pain in the arse to navigate.

I slowly made my way back into the inn, cursing myself for not bringing my water skin as I became out of breath, and made my way back towards the gates.

The streets here were so much livelier than the Behemoth's Claw and, despite how many people there were, I spotted a group of small children playing a game with a ball, skilfully throwing it to one and other over people's heads.

"This would be a lovely little place to live, I reckon," I mumbled, smiling.

And I imagined you'd get used to navigating this place pretty quick anyway.

Maybe when I retire, I really will move here one day.

That doesn't sound half bad.

"A lonely wanderer, hundreds of miles from home; sadness does he carry, burdened and tired is he, is this where you have found your journey's end?"

I stopped, turned to the side and, in an alleyway, sat against a building, was a frail looking old man with a rotten wooden stick in his hands. He had a thin black cloth over his eyes and only a few thin strands of long white hair on his head. His body was so skinny that I could see his bones pressing against his skin, threatening to pierce it.

He looked so deathly ill you'd be forgiven for mistaking him for a zombie.

A lot of his skin was an unnatural black, like it had been burnt or become infected by a terrible illness, and what remained of his original skin colour was scarred and cut.

"Excuse me?" I asked.

"A lonely wandered, hundreds of miles from home; sadness does he carry, burdened and tired is he, is this where you have found your journey's end?"

"...Who are you?"

"A question for a question, an answer for an answer; a traveller for a traveller," the old man said. "Adventurer, does the soldier's toil and pain not interest thee?"

...What the fuck?

How does he-?

"I-I don't-"

"How does he know us? Or can he see? Perhaps he is a spy sent to monitor thee? None of these I am, traveller, not I. I am a merchant but no goods nor coin do I have to give, or desire, from thee."

"...Then what are you a merchant of?"

"Words and truths, no lies or deceits. I only see the world for what it truly is and nothing else. I see no fog nor clouds, only clear days and skies. I felt your pain, your desires, your agony; the truth I can offer thee, if thee only but listen."

I don't know what to make of this.

He knew of Wiatt and I.

There's no way he could tell from listening alone, but maybe he was senile and said this to everyone who passed him.

I looked to my sides to see if anyone else around me had noticed, but no one else seemed to pay much attention to us, almost as if we didn't exist.

Maybe I was imagining this, or maybe this was like the experience I had with the Passageway in Itztli.

Perhaps, to the rest of the world, we really weren't there.

The blind man spoke the truth though.

I always wanted to know about Wiatt's past, especially now that I could call him friend. But, even after our journey together and everything we've been through, I thought that I truly knew nothing about him.

I had always suspected that Wiatt was a deserter from the Imperial army the moment I met him, but I had always been too afraid to ask him if he was what I thought. This old man said he was and spoke truthfully about my worries and how many questions were floating constantly through my mind.

Why did he run away from the Imperial army?

Was it because he thought they'd lose the war, or was it something else?

And if that was the case, why was he so eager to rush through the Narrow?

The Imperials wouldn't send soldiers into the Narrow to catch a single man, unless he had committed some serious crime or perhaps if he was a well-known noble, maybe even royalty, who had betrayed his country and fled.

Back when we couldn't enter Ehecatl, Wiatt had been incredibly impatient and wanted to continue our journey as quickly as he could.

Now that I think about it, it was strange how he didn't let me tend to his wounds he got from fighting the bandits after we killed them.

He refused to remove his shirt and, that night at the herbalists, he had yelled at the man.

I just didn't ever want to start coming up with theories behind his actions before I had actually asked him about it, for I might not trust his answers when he finally told them because of what I thought his reasons were.

If this man could truly see such things, should I ask him about it?

"Your answer you have found, your determination you have gained; ask him of what concerns you, ask him of why he acts. Tonight, you will find them; tonight, you shall see all. Wanderer and soldier, two souls of the same star, two souls that will drift afar; you shall both find you answers, tonight, and, come tomorrow, a new sun will rise for you."

I looked up at the old man once he had finished speaking and…

…he was gone…

Did I just get cursed or something?

Or is this what happens to priests or monks when they have divine revelations?

Please be the latter!

Please, Gods, let it be the latter!

…Best not to think too much about it.

After that, I headed back to the inn and had dinner. Wiatt joined me not too long afterwards and we sat largely in silence, only sharing pleasantries with one another and a few throwaway comments about our days.

Even though we had been talking like normal earlier in the day.

Though in truth, I think both of us had forced ourselves to act like normal.

We were both running away from what had happened in our own way and, once we saw one another again, we remembered our troubles and the mood turned awkward again.

So, as we sat there after finishing our dinner and drinking our ale, I decided to try and break the tension that had risen up between us again.

"Fancy a drinking game, lad?" I asked.

As embarrassing as this is to admit, my voice fucking broke as I spoke and I almost tripped over my words.

He looked at me, smiled, and said, "Sure."

Then, neither of us said anything for a few seconds.

Even though I had suggested it, I had no idea where the Depths to start.

"I'll go first then," Wiatt said, resting his elbows on the table. He hummed for a few seconds, then said, "What's your best childhood memory?"

I gave him a weird look. "I thought I'd told you, hadn't I?"

"Oh. You mean, the bard's stories, right?"

"Yeah. Um, what about you?"

Wiatt let out a small sigh. "…I don't have too many good memories of my childhood, sir."

Shit.

Shit!

Shit!

I shouldn't have asked!

Even though it was his question!

Okay, Athellio, things will get awkward if you don't change the topic with your next question.

So, Gods, please give me a divine revelation!

Let your words come from my mouth and divert this conversation as far away from this as possible!

"...Then...what's your worst...childhood...memory...?" I asked.

...I.

Am.

A.

Fucking.

Moron!

He looked at me, his smile returning, and he let out a loud laugh that, one that I'd never heard him make before.

"Athellio, you are something else, you know?" He said, wiping a tear from his eye.

"I'm sorry?"

"Don't be, sir." He laughed a little bit more. "Oh Gods, I needed to laugh like that again." His usual smile returned to his face. "That was a good joke, sir."

I grinned and chuckled myself. "Thought you might like it."

Somehow, he took it that way and not the dumb arse way I actually meant.

Wiatt took a big swig of his drink. "So, sir, what's your actual question?"

Shit!

"Well then," I said, leaning onto the table. "Is there anything at all about home you miss?"

"That I miss?"

"Or, just, you know, what's your favourite thing about home?"

"Oh Gods, where do I start?" Wiatt wondered.

"Too many to pick or too few?"

We laughed together. "Too many," he said.

"You said you lived in Titus, right? Did you grow up there?"

"I did, in the Coal Quarter. My dad was a guard in the city and began teaching me how to swing a sword from the age of four. My mum was a barmaid and they'd met after his shift while she was working."

"The Coal Quarter?"

"You've never heard of it, sir?"

I shook my head.

Truth be told, my knowledge of the city of Titus was severely lacking. I didn't know that there was a Coal Quarter, nor did I even know any of the other Quarter names in the city.

The only thing I did know was that, following the unification of Carlen, Titus had a gigantic stone statue of himself built outside the palace gates in the city.

I've heard it stands close to a hundred feet tall.

Unfortunately, however, I never got to visit Titus during my time in the Westerlands due to the high *'admission'* fee the guards tried to charge me.

Wiatt smiled somewhat sadly at me and said, "I guess it wouldn't be common knowledge to anyone outside of the city, let alone someone from the Green."

"…I just got hit with the strongest sense of déjà vu," I whispered.

"So did I, sir."

"What's it like in the Coal Quarter?"

"Boring, dirty and poor. We didn't have the most money, but we still had a happy enough life there, I guess."

…You guess?

"Is it an industrial part of the city?" I asked.

"Fairly. We have a lot of blacksmiths, tanners and craftsmen in the Quarter, but so do a lot of the other outlying districts. The Marble Quarter is where the palace and the nobility live."

"Could you ever go and visit it?"

He shook his head. "I tried, sir, a few times in fact, but they wouldn't let people in unless they were guards, soldiers, merchants, nobles or guests of the nobility. There's no way someone like me from the Coal Quarter would ever have been allowed in."

"…I see."

Wiatt shook his head. "It is what it is. The Empire's long since been divided between its classes, so it's hardly a surprise they'd stop the *'filth'* from seeing the beauty of the Marble Quarter." He grunted. "Well, if the rebels take the city, it might not look so glamorous anymore."

"Damn. Then I guess neither of us will get to see it then."

"Not until after the war, I reckon."

"…Yeah."

"But if I had to pick a favourite thing about home, it'd honestly be the Ruby Quarter."

"The Ruby one?"

Wiatt smiled slyly at me and, after a few seconds of processing what colour a ruby was, I think I figured out what he was getting at.

"Wish you'd told me about that twenty years ago," I mumbled.

Wiatt let out a hearty chuckle. "I would've been shorter than the table back then and if they let me into the brothels at that age, I think the whole city would've rioted."

"Perhaps."

"What about you, sir?" He asked.

"They'd have rioted for me, too."

Wiatt laughed. "Not that, sir. What's your favourite thing about home?"

"Sarah."

"Sarah, sir? Oh!" His eyes widened. "Is that her name?"

"Yeah, she's my-"

"Then, what's your favourite part of your wife?"

"First, she's my fiancé, not my wife. Not yet, anyway. Second, her kind heart."

"Aw, that's so sweet," Wiatt said with a smile; his expression turned deadpan. "But seriously, what you're favourite part of her?"

"Her kind hea-"

"Favourite part of her body?"

I looked away from him.

"…Her kind-"

He coughed.

I looked back to him.

Yep. He ain't buying it.

So, I answered honestly.

"…Her eyes."

"Her eyes, sir?"

I smiled. "They're a beautiful green, and, when she's happy, they sparkle. Honestly, it soothes me looking into them when they're like that."

…Well, the last time I saw them, they weren't anything like that.

I wonder what they'll look like when I next see her.

"You know, sir, when you give such a serious answer like that, I can't really say anything about it," Wiatt said with a small laugh.

"Sorry, lad, but the truth's the truth," I replied.

"Well, as I asked the last question, it's your turn now."

"Hmm." I leant back in my chair, a sly smirk on my lips, and hummed. "What to pick, what to pick."

"You can ask me anything, sir, and I'll tell you the truth."

Anything, eh?

…I wonder?

You shall both find your answers, tonight or tomorrow, and a new sun will rise for you.

If what that old man said was true, then now was the time to ask the question that had always been on my mind, since the first day I met Wiatt and my desire to ask had only grown with each and every passing moment along our journey.

Six words, that was all it was.

Six whole words that could destroy our friendship if I asked it.

When I thought about it like that, I honestly wanted to laugh.

"What are you hiding from me?"

It was that strange feeling again.

The feeling of the entire world coming to a standstill and all sound vanished in an instant.

If the old man was to be believed, then I would finally get the answers I always wanted to know.

After what felt like an eternity, Wiatt put down his drink, a thin smile across his lips.

"...When did you start feeling that way?" He asked.

He didn't even try to deny it.

"I knew you were hiding something from the beginning, but I didn't know what," I said. "Depths, even now all I have are theories and ideas, nothing concrete. I just knew you were hiding things. Like your story about your dad; you changed it. You told me weeks ago he was a librarian, not a guard. Don't know why you'd lie like that, but I guess you had your reasons for it; I just don't know what those are.

"The biggest thing though was when we fought those bandits. Your refusal about me treating your wounds and even just lifting up your shirt.; I have no idea why you'd say that unless you were hiding something big."

"...Can I refuse to answer, Athellio?"

I looked directly into his eyes and shook my head. "No."

"I see," he said. He took a big swig from his ale and then stared off to the side. "It's quite a long story, so please pay attention to it."

"My full name is Wiatt Lythers; I am the first son of Lord Ian Lythers, Prime Minister of the Empire of Carlen. Less than a year ago, I was a captain in the Imperial army and fought alongside my father against bandits, but, then the Emperor ordered us to do something horrific that caused the whole world to go to shit; he asked us to attack nobles who were Children of the Stars.

"...We kick started this war.

"At the time, my father had me convinced we were doing the right thing, telling me that the Emperor's spies had discovered a vast conspiracy that threatened to destroy the whole empire and the only way to stop it was to strike hard and fast against those involved. In the beginning, we only went after the nobles, their soldiers and their families." He grunted. "'*Necessary causalities*', my father said.

"But we didn't stop there.

"When the local populace found out what we'd done to their liege lords, they rioted and my fath-...Ian Lythers...ordered us to slaughter them. They had no weapons, no armour, no defences and they'd done nothing but protest against our crimes. I begged my father not to do this, to tell them the truth we'd discovered and show them we are doing the right thing, but he yelled and struck me, saying I was pitying traitors.

"So...my father's men attacked the village, killing and burning anything that they could. I was horrified by what I was seeing but, to stop my father from getting any ideas of killing me as a sympathiser to the enemy, I pretended to go along with the attack. I charged into the village screaming and yelling like the rest and, once I was out of his sight, I stopped and cursed my own weakness.

"People were dying all around me and I was powerless to do anything to stop them.

"I had intended to stay hidden somewhere during the slaughter and cover my ears and shut my eyes, but then I saw three of our men drag a young girl into a farmhouse, tearing at her clothes." He clenched his fists and a nasty scowl appeared on his face. "I wasn't going to let that happen.

"I charged them and stabbed one in the back. The other two went for their swords, but I cut down one before he could draw his blade; the other managed to slice at me." Wiatt pointed to the scar on his cheek. "He's the one who gave me this. So, I cut off his head.

"The girl, Gods bless her heart, was terrified and crying, and all I could do was tell her to find somewhere to hide until this is all over. When she didn't seem able to walk, I held out my hand and offered to help her. Her whole body shook as she reached for my hand and then." He grimaced. "I heard someone scream and running behind me. I turned to face them and got stabbed in the stomach.

"Not by one of our men, but by a villager.

"He screamed *'Get away from my sister!'* and went to stab me again, but she managed to leap to my defence, shouting that I had saved her. The scared lad took a moment to look at everything in the barn and realised how he'd gotten the situation wrong and helped tend to my wounds with his sister. After a few minutes of rough treatment, I told them to hide themselves and run as soon as they could away from this place.

"They thanked me and apologised for the wound in my gut, but I told them not to.

"All I did was one tiny act of good amidst a gigantic, horrific act of cruelty.

"I walked out of the barn and re-joined my father. He asked me where I had been, but didn't press any further when I showed him my bloodied blade and said that some of our men had been killed by villagers. I said that I finished them off; he seemed satisfied with that, though I think he could tell I was hiding something and had been wounded.

"Even though the villagers had tried their best to aid me, there was no way they could hide the cut on my cheek.

"When we returned to the capital, all the way from the Coal Quarter to the Marble, we were hailed as heroes under a false banner of executing traitors though, even then, I could tell just how many of the populace hated us and heard what we'd done. My father was eating it up though. I don't think I've ever seen him so happy.

"When we got back to the mansion, I checked the wound in my gut and saw just how bad it really had become. It was purple and yellow, like it had been infected with the worst disease imaginable, and puss was leaking from it. I didn't understand it at first and thought that a small rusty knife wound would be nothing, but." He chuckled. "I had no idea how wrong I was.

"I called doctors, herbalists and mages to inspect the wound, in private and without my father's knowledge, but none of them could figure out what exactly was wrong with it. The doctors and herbalists thought it to be an infection, but none of their usual cures or treatments worked. The mages tried to heal it, but nothing worked. I even went to the Church and asked them to bless and purify it, but it didn't work.

"My wound was getting worse and worse as the days went by and, soon enough, I had no other options left. None. Except, for one, thin, desperate, foolish hope.

"Since I was young, I had been an avid reader and our family's library was filled with hundreds of texts, some of which no one else in the entire world had. I would spend my evenings in there many days after training and Alfyr's writings on the Narrow had always fascinated me. Once I had no options left to turn to, I went to the library to look for something, anything that could help or, at the very least, point me in the right direction.

"Then, when I saw Alfyr's notes, I remembered Toci, the City of Healers, and thought *'If nothing else can cure it, what about the legendary healers of the Narrow?'* Toci's healing springs are said to be able to cure any wound and restore life to anyone, even those a second from death, and so I beseeched my father to give me leave to tend to my wounds.

"He forbade me and said that I would fight to the bitter end against the Emperor's enemies until they were all dead and then, once that was done, I could heal my wounds. I was furious and, had I been even more foolish than I am, I might have cut him down there and then. If I had, I'd definitely have been killed, so I instead decided to escape in the middle of the night with my father's Star Sword and, in disguise, rode for the Narrow as fast as I could.

"I avoided every single Imperial settlement, patrol route, often visited roads, taverns and forts, and was heartbroken when I got to Yarthan and saw the ports were closed. They were going to be my way out of the Westerlands originally and I had hoped to make it on a ship before they sealed the border. Unfortunately, I had to go with my secondary plan of sneaking through the south and into the Narrow, but I was scared to venture along that path alone.

"And then, I saw you drinking by yourself in that tavern and knew instantly that you were just like me; someone desperate to get as far away from the Westerlands as soon as possible. After that, well, you know the rest. Well, to an extent. I didn't let you properly bandage my wounds because I didn't want you to see what is killing me and…yeah…that's everything."

I didn't say anything for what felt like years, processing everything that he had just told me.

And, after all that time and thinking, all I could say was what I truly felt in my heart at that moment.

"Everything you told me about you was a lie," I whispered, dumbfounded. "Everything."

"Not everything."

I snorted. "Okay, so you told the truth about Alfyr's writings. Fucking fantastic, lad, truly. I thought you were just a deserter or maybe an adventurer or merc who'd fucked with the wrong people, not the son of the second most powerful family in the Westerlands." I shook my head in disbelief. "...That's not even the most unbelievable thing."

"...What's the most-?"

"The fact that you didn't tell me you were dying!"

I'm pretty sure my shout caught the attention of some nearby tables and, worse, some of them stopped talking after I yelled, no doubt to listen in.

But I was far too pissed off to care.

"...I'm sorry," he whispered.

"Sorry?" I repeated. "Sorry? Sorry doesn't even begin to cut it. If I'd know that, then I would've made sure we made it through the Narrow as quickly as possible. We'd be at Toci already, you'd be cured and we'd all live happily ever after. Now, it turns out, you'd be lucky if you just survived."

"Why are you getting so angry about this?"

"Why?!"

"Yes, why?"

"Because you're my friend and if you're dying then of course I don't want that to happen! Why are you so relaxed about this? You could've dropped dead at any point in our journey and-"

"But I didn't!" He shouted back. "I've survived this long and I could survive for even longer or, Depths, I could drop dead right now for all that it matters."

"For all it matters?"

"Yes! If I'm going to die tomorrow or in the night, then I am going to act like today is my last day alive and live as happily as possible!"

He sighed and slumped back into his chair. "This is why I didn't want to tell you."

"But you insisted we went faster. When we couldn't enter Ehecatl, you were very upset and angry, weren't you?" I asked.

"I was. Of course I was."

"But...If you didn't care about your own life-"

"I never said that, did I?" I stared at him, truly confused. "I don't want to die, far from it. Life's too short already and having an incurable infection in my stomach slowly eating away at my life is scary. Every night, I don't know if I'll wake up and, every time I feel the wound begin to burn, I start to wonder if I'll just drop dead where I stand and that'll be it. So, I wanted to heal myself, but I didn't want to spend my last few weeks just travelling as fast as I could on the slim chance that I could survive.

"If I was going to die or had the chance to just fall over and die at any moment, then I wanted to live my life to the fullest and make the most of what little time I had left. So, I wanted to emphasise speed and enjoyment as we travelled and that we did.

"Athellio, these last few weeks have honestly been some of the best of my life. Every city we saw was amazing, every day I felt like I was experiencing something knew and even when there were times we almost died, I still enjoyed myself."

"…That's why you entered Xolotl," I said coldly. "You thought you could die at any point and wanted to do something reckless and thrilling, right?"

He smiled weakly and nodded. "You know me well, Athellio."

"No. No, I don't. I thought I did, I really did…turns out I didn't."

"Well, I'm sure you'll understand this. I didn't want to undertake this journey just to save my life; I did it because I wanted to see the beauty and wonder of the Narrow before I died. So, I wanted to see as much as possible, do as much as possible and enjoy my life as much as possible."

I shook my head. "That's dumb."

"I know it is, but I don't want to change the way I think ever, even when I get this wound fixed," Wiatt said with a bright smile. "You shouldn't worry about my life, Athellio."

"That's a lot to ask."

He laughed a little. "I guess it might be." Wiatt quickly finished his drink and stood up. "Honestly, I don't mind if I die tonight, tomorrow or the day after as long as I can feel like I'm alive today."

At that comment, I couldn't help but find myself smile bitterly at both of us.

That approach to life was exactly the same as mine.

The life of an adventurer, only caring about the current day they were living in, seeking the next big, brilliant, wonderful adventure and not interested in life beyond that.

…That was my life right now.

"…Did you even give any thought to what you'd do once you were cured?" I asked. Wiatt shook his head. "Maybe give it some thought, maybe try writing stuff you want to do with your life tonight before bed…just, you know…"

Wiatt smiled and nodded. "I know. I'll try."

"…Goodnight, Wiatt," I said.

"…Goodnight, Athellio."

He left me alone to finish up my drink and I stayed at the table a little while after I was done, my mind lost in a sea of thoughts.

The old man had been right; I'd found my answers and, with it, I found even more questions that I had to ask myself.

Though, poor lad, he doesn't even know what exactly about his wound is killing him.

No one could figure it out, no one could help him, no one could cure him.

It's almost like he was being punished by the Gods.

Perhaps he was, for being a part of those horrific crimes in the Westerlands, even as a bystander.

Or maybe that's exactly why they were punishing him?

He hadn't stopped it and hadn't done enough to try and stop it, so the Gods were damning him for his part in it.

If that was the case, then the Star Rebellion would succeed and the Empire of Carlen would fall.

If that was their will, that is.

Still, tonight, there was nothing I could do about it other than worry and wonder.

I finished my drink, went up into my room and climbed into my bed, though I found myself staring blankly at the ceiling for a long time.

What stuck with me though wasn't the fact that Wiatt was dying, but it was his reckless way that he handled his life.

Living just for the thrill of the day, not caring at all about what comes tomorrow and things like that.

Still, I couldn't criticise him.

It's how I had lived my life.

Depths, it was how I'm living my life right now and I hate it.

I hate being on the road every day. I hate never getting to sleep in my own bed in my own home with my fiancé. I hate not staying in the same place for more than a month unless I'm wounded or sick.

I grunted.

"What a terrible way to live," I mumbled.

You shall both find you answers, tonight, and, come tomorrow, a new sun will rise for you.

Something hit me.

A divine revelation of sorts.

…I…am an idiot.

I have been an idiot this entire time.

Ever since I started travelling through the Narrow, my mind and heart had always wandered off to the same place, they had always, always kept her in my thoughts and no matter how hard I tried to push them down, they kept coming back up again and again.

...I didn't want to be an adventurer anymore...

That lifestyle wasn't what I wanted anymore and I only realised that by seeing how dumb it was myself in Wiatt.

He was acting just like I would and it pissed me off.

This was exactly the same feeling that Sarah went through every time I came home and she saw me off.

Maybe it was worse for her.

Truth be told, she would have no way of knowing if I died right now or if I left her for another woman, or if I drowned at sea or if I got imprisoned and left to rot.

She could only believe that I would come back to her every time I left.

I put my head in my hands and began to weep.

Gods, what have I done...?

Oh Gods...

I don't want that.

I don't want to die a thousand miles from her and leave her alone for the rest of her life.

I want to settle down.

I want to start a family.

I want to live a life where I can go home every night and see my beautiful wife and my little kids running up excitedly when they see me.

I want that.

I don't want to live my life on the road anymore.

I just want her in my life.

Sarah, please, please have waited for me this one last time...

Now's not the time to cry!

I wiped my eyes and collected myself.

I have to get home and quickly!

I have to see her, drop onto one knee, ask her to be mine and that I can be hers, and that she can somehow find it in her heart to forgive me.

Wait for me, my wife.

I couldn't help but chuckle and smile when I thought that.

I'll finally be getting married to the woman I love and, until I finally fell asleep, I couldn't stop grinning like an absolute idiot.

CHAPTER ELEVEN

When I awoke, I leapt out of bed, washed my face, got dressed and then went out to the balcony to take a deep breath of the morning air..

I felt so refreshed after yesterday, in a lot of ways.

I finally got the answers I wanted from Wiatt and I finally found what I wanted to do with my life.

All that was left now was just to make it home and make it happen.

I got changed and gathered my things before heading downstairs to get some breakfast and meet with Wiatt.

I wondered if he wouldn't be there before me this time because of everything that we discussed last night, but, like usual, he was waiting for me already.

We spoke without ever mentioning the events of the night before.

We had breakfast, gave the innkeeper a well earnt tip, which Wiatt paid himself using his remaining coin, got our horses and promptly left the city.

Toci was less than three days from Atlaua and, without so much as a word to one another, we hastened our pace so that we might make it in half that time, provided there were no unforeseen circumstances to get in our way.

And, for the first time in our journey, we didn't speak of the next city we were going to.

"So, lad, did ya give any more thought to what you want to do after your wounds are healed?" I asked.

"Hmm, to be honest, I still haven't really got an idea of what to do next," Wiatt answered with a faint smile.

"Truly?"

"Truly. I stayed up until the early hours of the morning with a parchment and quill trying to think of something, anything, I could write to do and say to myself, *'That's what I want to do!'*, but, alas, I found nothing. Maybe it's because I don't really know what's waiting for me afterwards."

"Life?"

Wiatt chuckled. "Not quite what I meant, sir. I guess it's more…I don't really know where I could go next, you know? I barely know anything about the Green and I don't have any coin to spend anymore."

"That last one's your own fault, you know."

"I know, I know, sir, but I guess I best find a job once we reach the Green."

"And a cave to sleep in."

Wiatt lowered his head and smiled weakly. "I forgot about that part as well."

I laughed at him and smacked him on the back. "Don't worry. I'll give ya a nice blanket and pillow before I go."

"...You know, you can be quite spiteful when you want to be."

"You ain't seen anything yet, lad."

We both laughed heartily and turned our attention back to the road before us.

"Maybe you could apply to be a guard in a city or town in the south," I suggested. "Not forever, of course, but maybe until you can get back on your own two feet."

"I have a feeling that I never would get back onto my feet if I did become a guard," Wiatt said.

"Why's that?"

"Sir, there's two things I know that guards definitely do: get bored and get drunk, the latter of which costs a fair bit of money from their small salary. If I'm lucky, after twenty years of service, I might be able to buy a small one room shack in the slums."

"Is that how bad it is in the Westerlands?"

Wiatt shot me a confused look. "Isn't that the case everywhere?"

I shook my head. "In the Green, most guards have enough to start a family, own a house and raise a few kids, and still have enough money to get pissed every night."

The lad's eyes widened. "That doesn't sound too bad."

Truth be told, I didn't know that for sure, but what harm would it do to give the kid a bit more hope for his future, eh?

"Ah, but aren't there a lot of corrupt guards in city watches?" Wiatt asked.

"Definitely."

"Hmm, maybe not then."

"Too scared of a few ruffians?"

"Too scared of the guys who'd pay those ruffians."

I nodded.

"Fair enough."

"Is there an adventurer's guild in the Green?" He asked.

"Several. And mercenary companies," I replied. "Those would definitely be your thing. Good pay, good ale, lots of women and lots of travelling."

Wiatt chuckled. "That doesn't sound too bad. Maybe I could do that for a while, earn a good amount of coin and we could go travelling together again one day. There are so many places around the world I'd love to see. The Eastern Province, the kingdoms of the Green. Depths, even the Sands would be lovely to see one day."

Wiatt, my friend, you should've asked me twenty years ago and I would've gone with you to any of those places and more.

"If you would have me sir, I would love to travel with you again someday," Wiatt said with his usual smile.

Gods know I haven't seen that bright smile in what feels like years. However.

"This was my last journey," I said, not meeting his eyes. "I'm done being an adventurer."

It took many seconds for Wiatt to speak up again once I had said that.

"...Truly, sir?" He asked in a voice that was almost a whisper.

I smiled at him. "Truly."

"But you seemed to enjoy our time together so much. Was it something I-?"

"Oi, I never said you were the problem, did I?"

"No, but-"

"Did you piss me off last night? Fuck yes. Did you piss me off when you charged into the city of death? Depths yes, you did. Do I hate you? Of course not." I snorted. "Maybe I should, all things considered, but I don't. I just hated seeing you waste your life like that."

"...Is it a waste to be an adventurer, sir?"

I stopped my horse and Wiatt stopped his.

"Do you think you wasted your life, sir?"

I sighed. "Honestly, I don't know myself. I loved being on the road., I loved seeing the Sands, the Eastern Province, the Nords of the North. I can't even begin to count the great and unthinkable things I've seen across the world in my time, and now I've been through the Narrow." I smiled thinly. "When I think of it like that, how could I not be happy with what I've done in my life?

"I mean, how many people can say that they've done the things that I have, seen the places I have, seen the people and monsters I have? I could probably count them on my fingers, but...I don't regret it, but I regret how much time I wasted, not how I used it."

Wiatt's expression twisted, like he didn't know how I really felt.

Or maybe he didn't know how he really felt.

"Nine years ago, I met Sarah and we fell in love so quickly that I wanted to marry her within a few months," I said. "But, every time I had the chance, every moment I could've come to her and just told her how I really felt, I...left. I went off on a grand adventure, promising her that I would return to her with riches beyond measures and stories to last a lifetime. Each time, when I left, she looked at me with such lonely, sad eyes and it hurt me to see them.

"As time went on, it became unbearable to even look at her as I left.

"Those eyes went from sad to cold, and from cold to empty.

"Those eyes…I still remember now…those were the ones she showed me this time…and when I think of it like that, it's hard for me to feel good about the time I've spent travelling far away from her. Yeah, I've seen so much of the beauty and wonder that the world has to offer, but that doesn't mean half as much as seeing her does.

"There's only one place in this world that I need to be more than anywhere else and that's home."

For minutes, we both sat there on our horses in silence, not moving, trying not to breathe too loudly and neither of us breaking eye contact with the other.

I didn't know what kind of face I was making, but Wiatt's face was painful to look at.

He seemed so confused, so hurt, so sad, and so surprised all at once.

Even then, as much as it hurt bringing my feelings out like that and seeing him look at me with that face, I didn't break eye contact until he did.

He looked down to his side, his lips curled into a small smile, and he said, "Okay."

Then, he loudly cleared his throat and started riding again. "Well, no sense in wasting anymore time here. Let's keep moving, shall we?"

"…Yeah," I mumbled, following after him.

***

"Lad," I said, not looking at him to see if he was still listening. "I don't want to be Athellio the Wanderer anymore; I just want to be Athellio."

Wiatt didn't say another word to me that day, nor did he say anything when I suggested we stop to camp for the night nor when we were about to sleep.

In the small cave that we had found, he had just sat near the fire, sword resting beside him and looking out of the cave.

It seemed he would be taking the first watch, with or without me saying so.

"Goodnight, Wiatt," I said, hoping he'd speak to me again.

Sadly, it didn't seem like he would be saying that to me.

So, I turned over and shut my eyes.

Before I drifted off that night, I could've sworn I heard Wiatt say something, but I only caught a few faint words before I slipped into darkness.

"…-ight, sir…I'm…but I don't have…-re…"

***

That night, Wiatt didn't wake me up when it was my turn to take watch.

Confused, I awoke at the crack of dawn to find the campfire extinguished and Wiatt asleep at the mouth of the cave on his side in an uncomfortable looking position.

Did he fall asleep and forget to-?

Shit!

No, no, no, no, no, no, no!

I quickly got up and ran over to him, shaking him.

"Wiatt! Wiatt, wake up! Wiatt!" I cried.

However, no matter how much I shook him, he didn't stir.

I touched my hand to his cheek and it was…ice cold.

"No…" I mumbled. "No, you can't be-! No!" I turned him onto his back and looked at his face; his eyes were closed and he was smiling. "Wiatt! Wiatt!"

I fell onto my knees beside my friend and smashed my fist into the ground, cursing so loudly it echoed through the cave multiple times.

I looked at his face and felt my eyes watering.

"Shit," I whispered, quickly drying my eyes.

We were half a day from the City of Healers and we had been too late.

CHAPTER TWELVE

With what little food and water we…I had left, I didn't have the time to properly bury Wiatt, but there was no way that I was going to leave him in a small, dank cave.

No way in Depths.

I carried Wiatt's body onto his horse, then rode both of our steeds to the waterside and I began gathering the biggest rocks and stones I could find. Once I had enough, I gently placed Wiatt's body on a cliff's edge twenty metres from the coast and began piling stones on top of him until he was completely buried by them.

I made sure that he was facing out towards the sea, towards his homeland and towards the vast, open world that he wished to explore.

I wanted him to at least see how big and beautiful the world was, even if it was only in death that he could see it.

I left him with all of his belongings and took only his sword.

I didn't want to desecrate his body even slightly.

More than three hundred miles from his home, this would be his final resting place and it was one that only I would ever know about.

Even if someone came across it, and I'm sure they would, they wouldn't know to whom the grave belonged to.

I also knew, deep in my heart, that someone would probably raid his grave, take his things and leave his body for the animals to pick away at, but I couldn't just leave him to that fate.

I had to at least try.

With my friend buried, I bent down and prayed over his grave in the way of the people of the Westerlands, then in the Narrow as we'd seen in the City of Gods, and then in the way people of the Green prayed.

I prayed to each and every God I knew, beseeched them all to watch over him, and to bring him happiness in his next life, if he is fortunate enough to be given one.

Even if he wasn't in their eyes, I begged them in my mind to give him one.

Once I had prayed for about ten minutes, I opened my eyes and sat before Wiatt's grave on my knees.

It was such a weird feeling, to be honest, saying goodbye to a friend that I hadn't known for even two months.

I was sad, of course, but I also felt…strange, for lack of a better word.

There was still so much that I wanted to say to him, so much more of the world I wished he could see and I wanted to help him start a new life in the Green.

If we had been just a bit faster, then he might still be alive and that life would have been his.

I blamed myself,

I knew it wasn't my fault though.

I didn't know he was dying and Wiatt himself admitted he could've picked up the pace, but I still felt something…lingering in my heart and mind.

"I still have so much to tell you, lad," I said softly, a faint smile on my lips. "I really do wish I could've spent more time with you. Depths, we had so much to talk about and…I never got to properly apologise to you. Truthfully, I don't know what it was like for you, how you felt, nor do I know what your life was like before I met you. I can imagine, but I don't think I could ever truly understand what you were going through.

"Though, what I can say for sure is I knew what it was like to be young, to want to go on adventurers, to see and experience great and fantastic things…and I had no right to judge you for how you lived your life. After all, I was just the same, once upon a time. And it was because of you, lad, that I was able to finally find what I wanted to do with my life and that is a debt I will never, ever be able to pay now.

"I couldn't even give you a proper burial. These stones were the best thing I could find and the nicest ones I could lift." I smiled bitterly. "Though, I'm sure you'd understand that."

I leant back and stared off across the ocean.

From where I had buried him, I could see in the distance a ship sailing northward towards the Green.

"We really were close, weren't we?" I mumbled.

I stood up, brushed myself down and turned back to the grave. "Thank you, Wiatt. You were a good friend and from the bottom of my heart I am honoured that you spent your last journey in this world with me. If the Gods are kind, perhaps we'll meet each other again in another life."

And with that, those last, painful, lingering regrets that I had begun to lift a little.

I guess I had said everything I needed to…even if it wasn't everything I wanted to.

I untied my horse from a tree, climbed onto it and began a fast ride towards the Green.

I was still half a day away from Toci and could've easily followed the Great Stone Road to it, or even further beyond that to the city of Oxomo and see their legendary scholars, but I didn't want to visit them any longer.

All I wanted to do was take the quickest path home and not wander from that path until I was back home and back with Sarah.

***

Even going as quickly as I did, it took me almost an entire week to make it back to Wheatcraft.

I was somehow shocked that the village hadn't changed even a little since I left.

It was the same.

The exact same, even down to the shit along the side of the road.

Though, I didn't care.

I road through the village towards our home, a quaint two-story house on a tiny hill towards the outskirts of the village. It was a beautiful little house that I had paid for with the funds from my adventures to build.

I wonder if Sarah's in, or if she's even still living here…

Hahaha, the Gods really do have a sick sense of humour.

I was too late to save Wiatt but I arrived at the right time to see Sarah at our house.

She had been tending to the garden at the front of our house as I pulled up on my horse.

She seemed almost dumbfounded that I had returned, not happy or sad, just…surprised.

"…Hey," I said with an awkward smile.

"…Hi," Sarah replied.

…Gods have mercy on me…

Her eyes look so empty when she looks at me.

"I'm-I'm home."

"I noticed."

She bent back down and continued watering the flowers.

Of course, she was pissed.

I would be too.

I climbed off my horse, tied it to the gate and walked towards her. "…Did any of my letters make it?"

"…No," she whispered.

"Right. I guess they didn't."

"…When are you off again?"

That hurt.

I knew it was coming and I deserved it, but it still didn't stop it from hurting.

But I was done running from this pain.

"…I'm not," I said.

She stopped watering the plants and then grunted. "I've heard that before."

"I mean it this time."

"I've heard that before, too."

"...I know you have, but, this time, I really do mean it, Sarah. I swear it."

Sarah put down the watering can, took off her gloves, stood up and spun to face me.

"Why in the Depths should I believe that?" She asked, frowning at me. "How many times have you said that and then just had *'One more adventure?'* or just found *'Something that you need to do?'* Do you even know how many times?"

"I-"

"I do. Seven. Seven times in nine years, Athellio. And every time like an idiot I believed you." She smiled sadly and shook her head. "You know, when I heard about the war over there, I thought you were dead when I didn't hear anything from you. Do you know how much I cried for you?"

I shook my head. "I can't even begin to imagine."

"Of course you can't. Because you never thought about it before, did you?"

"...I did, but-"

"But what? You valued being *'The Wanderer'* more?" She clicked her tongue and turned back to the flowers. "Why do I ever get my hopes up with you? You know the number of people in this village who have tried to get me to move on from you? Almost all of them, but I never could."

...Shit, I can hear her sobbing.

"Even after everything, I still loved you and couldn't do it, and you still keep doing this same thing to me time and time again," she said, almost like she was cursing my very existence. "If you're going to just say it for the sake of it, then-"

"I'll prove it."

Sarah turned to look at me as I walked over to the road to a young lad I saw passing by that I knew fairly well.

Actually, he seemed less like he was walking by and running right up to me.

"Good day, Mr. Athellio!" The young lad called to me.

"Good day, William," I called back. "How did you know I was back in Wheatcraft?"

"My Pa saw you as you came back and told me. Said you'd probably head right home."

I smiled brightly.

Is this another blessing from the Gods?

Right when I needed someone, he appeared, almost like it was meant to be.

"Hey, lad, how old are you now?"

"I'll be eighteen next month, Mr. Athellio!" He said happily. "I'd love for you to come and celebrate with us down at the inn, if you'll be-"

"I'll be there." William's face lit up. "Your Pa give his blessing for you to go travelling?"

"Aye."

"Then, you'll need these."

Without another word, I started unstrapping my leather armour, starting with my chest piece, and handed them to him one by one. William was saying things to me, no doubt protesting or saying that he couldn't possibly take it, but I didn't listen.

Once I had done that, I then took my own sword off my belt and handed it to him.

"Mr. Athellio?" He shyly asked.

"I got hurt on my last journey," I said to him. "I can't be an adventurer any more. This stuff would be wasted on me."

"I'm sorry to hear that, but are you-?"

"Consider it a birthday present." I winked at him. "An early one." He opened his mouth to object but I thrust my sword into his palm. "May it serve you as well as it served me."

William still looked a little confused and shy, but then nodded and smiled as best he could. "I'm honoured. Thank you, Mr. Athellio. Will you be at the tavern tonight?"

"Might be. Depends on…things."

"Then, tomorrow night, could we drink together?"

"Of course."

William smiled and then said, "Thank you. Oh, I best get back. Goodbye, Mr. Athellio!"

"Good luck, William!" I called to him as he ran off.

Whenever I returned to the village, William would always sit by me and ask me about my adventures, ask me to tell him stories and he'd talk about his dreams to go adventuring one day.

It wasn't going to be an easy, or even a happy life to live, but it was his to live and I didn't want to take his dream away from him.

Depths, even if I told him not to go, he'd still go and risk his life so, at the very least, it's best to make sure he at least has gear to protect himself.

I gave him all of my prized and treasured equipment, including the armour that I had worn since I was eighteen.

I gave him everything, everything except for Wiatt's sword.

That I won't ever give up.

I turned back to our house and saw Sarah looking at me dumbstruck, her mouth agape, and staring blankly at me.

"You were right, Sarah. I'll never know how much it hurt you, and I'll never know how many times I made you cry and feel like shit. And it's because of that that I want to give up my life as an adventurer and settle down with you. I want you to be my wife. I want to have children, raise a family and…" I smiled and reached to my necklace, pulling off the ring I'd bought weeks ago in Chicomecoatl. "I want to be with you forever."

"…You really won't go away again?" She asked, taking a step closer to me.

"…I won't."

She took more steps towards me. "You won't go on another adventure a thousand miles from me?"

I shook my head and smiled. "I don't plan on leaving you for the rest of my life."

She was now right before me, looking up into my eyes.

"…You really mean it this time?"

I nodded. "…I do." Then, I held out my palm and she put her hand on mine. I slid the ring onto her ring finger and kissed her forehead.

Sarah's eyes began to water and she tightly embraced me, clutching onto me and digging her hands into my back. I held her back and stroked her hair lovingly.

"…I swear to all the Gods that if you're lying to me, I'll never forgive you," she said into my shoulder. "This is your last chance, you know?"

"I know, but I won't need another chance after this one," I whispered.

We kissed each other and stayed holding one another until Sarah had calmed down.

That night, we shared a bed together again and swore to each other our love, and agreed to be married as soon as we could.

Sarah fell asleep on my body and I held her close, smiling at her sleeping face and I lightly stroked her cheek. She squirmed a little in her sleep but subconsciously rubbed her cheek against my hand.

Gods, how I missed this.

I smiled and my eyes turned upwards to the ceiling.

Wiatt, if I had never met you and gone on that last, grand, dangerous, beautiful and terrifying adventure with you, I never would've discovered what I truly wanted in life and I'm forever in your debt.

I can only lament that I won't be able to pay that back in this life.

If you can hear me, Wiatt, thank you.

The End.

AUTHOR BIOGRAPHY

Daniel Christopher Priest (D.C. Priest) was born on the 7th November 1996 in the county of Hertfordshire and has been actively writing since he was 12 years old. *A Traveller in the Narrow* is his 2nd published work after *The Gold Crusade* and he has a degree in Creative and Professional Writing from Bangor University. He has a great passion for writing, reading, history, myths, legends and fantasy.

Printed in Great Britain
by Amazon